DEATH BY VIOLENCE

Sally, beautiful little Sally, was there
staring down at the cord tied
neatly around the man's neck.

"Look," Archie said, "he's dead."

"Dead . . ."

"Yeah. D-E-A-D. Strangled."

"I think I'll go home," Sally said.

"Oh, no, you won't," Archie told his client.
"You'll walk out that door. You will get in a
taxicab. You will go straight to
Nero Wolfe."

GAMBIT

Nero Wolfe's fascinating game of wits
with a brilliant killer.

Books by Rex Stout

THE SILENT SPEAKER
TOO MANY WOMEN
AND BE A VILLAIN
TROUBLE IN TRIPLICATE
MURDER BY THE BOOK
TRIPLE JEOPARDY
THE GOLDEN SPIDERS
THREE MEN OUT
THE BLACK MOUNTAIN
BEFORE MIDNIGHT
THREE WITNESSES
MIGHT AS WELL BE DEAD
THREE FOR THE CHAIR
IF DEATH EVER SLEPT
AND FOUR TO GO
CHAMPAGNE FOR ONE
PLOT IT YOURSELF
THE SECOND CONFESSION
THREE AT WOLFE'S DOOR
TOO MANY CLIENTS
IN THE BEST FAMILIES
THE FINAL DEDUCTION
PRISONER'S BASE

Published by Bantam Books

A NERO WOLFE NOVEL

GAMBIT

BY REX STOUT

*This low-priced Bantam Book
has been completely reset in a type face
designed for easy reading, and was printed
from new plates. It contains the complete
text of the original hard-cover edition.*
NOT ONE WORD HAS BEEN OMITTED.

GAMBIT

*A Bantam Book / published by arrangement with
The Viking Press, Inc.*

PRINTING HISTORY
*Viking edition published October 1962
Bantam edition published February 1964*

*Bantam Books are published by Bantam Books, Inc. Its trade-mark,
consisting of the words "Bantam Books" and the portrayal of a
bantam, is registered in the United States Patent Office and in other
countries. Marca Registrada. Printed in the United States of Amer-
ica. Bantam Books, Inc., 271 Madison Ave., New York 16, N. Y.*

1

At twenty-seven minutes past eleven that Monday morning in February, Lincoln's Birthday, I opened the door between the office and the front room, entered, shut the door, and said, "Miss Blount is here."

Without turning his head Wolfe let out a growl, yanked out some more pages and dropped them on the fire, and demanded, "Who is Miss Blount?"

I tightened my lips and then parted them to say, "She is the daughter of Matthew Blount, president of the Blount Textile Corporation, who is in the coop charged with murder, and she has an appointment with you at eleven-thirty, as you know. If you're pretending you've forgotten, nuts. You knew you couldn't finish that operation in half an hour. Besides, how about the comments I have heard you make about book burners?"

"They are not relevant to this." He yanked out more pages. "I am a man, not a government or a committee of censors. Having paid forty-seven dollars and fifty cents for this book, and having examined it and found it subversive and intolerably offensive, I am destroying it." He dropped the pages on the fire. "I'm in no mood to listen to a woman. Ask her to come after lunch."

"I have also heard you comment about people who dodge appointments they have made."

Pause. More pages. Then: "Very well. Bring her here."

I returned to the office, shutting the door, crossed to the red leather chair near the end of Wolfe's desk where I had seated the caller, and faced her. She tilted her head back to look up at me. She was a brownie, not meaning a Girl Scout —small ears and a small nose, big brown eyes, a lot of brown

1

hair, and a wide mouth that would have been all right with the corners turned up instead of down.

"I'd better explain," I told her. "Mr. Wolfe is in the middle of a fit. It's complicated. There's a fireplace in the front room, but it's never lit because he hates open fires. He says they stultify mental processes. But it's lit now because he's using it. He's seated in front of it, on a chair too small for him, tearing sheets out of a book and burning them. The book is the new edition, the third edition, of Webster's New International Dictionary, Unabridged, published by the G. & C. Merriam Company of Springfield, Massachusetts. He considers it subversive because it threatens the integrity of the English language. In the past week he has given me a thousand examples of its crimes. He says it is a deliberate attempt to murder the—I beg your pardon. I describe the situation at length because he told me to bring you in there, and it will be bad. Even if he hears what you say, his mental processes are stultified. Could you come back later? After lunch he may be human."

She was staring up at me. "He's burning up a *dictionary?*"

"Right. That's nothing. Once he burned up a cookbook because it said to remove the hide from a ham end before putting it in the pot with lima beans. Which he loves most, food or words, is a tossup."

"I don't want to come back." She stood up. "I want to see him now. I *must* see him now."

The trouble was, if I persuaded her to put it off she might not show again. When she had phoned for an appointment it had looked as if we were going to have Matthew Blount for a client, and, judging from the newspapers and the talk around town, he could use plenty of good detective work; and he could pay for it, even at Nero Wolfe's rates. So I didn't want to shoo her out, and also there was her face—not only the turned-down corners of her mouth, but the look in her eyes. There is trouble in the eyes of nearly everyone who comes to that office, but hers were close to desperate. If I eased her out she might go straight to some measly agency with no genius like Wolfe and no dog like me.

"Okay, but I told you," I said, and went to my desk for my notebook, stepped to the door to the front room, and opened it. She came, leaving her coat, pallid mink, on the back of the chair.

I moved up chairs for us, but with Wolfe so close to the

fireplace I couldn't put her directly facing him. He rarely stands when a caller enters, and of course he didn't then, with the dictionary, the two-thirds of it that was left, on his lap. He dropped sheets on the fire, turned to look at her, and inquired, "Do you use 'infer' and 'imply' interchangeably, Miss Blount?"

She did fine. She said simply, "No."

"This book says you may. Pfui. I prefer not to interrupt this auto-da-fé. You wish to consult me?"

"Yes. About my father. He is in—he has been arrested for murder. Two weeks ago a man died, he was poisoned—"

"If you please. I read newspapers. Why do you come to me?"

"I know my father didn't do it and I want you to prove it."

"Indeed. Did your father send you?"

"No."

"Did his attorney, Mr. Kalmus?"

"No, nobody sent me. Nobody knows I'm here. I have twenty-two thousand dollars here in my bag." She patted it, brown leather with straps, on her lap. "I didn't have that much, but I sold some things. I can get more if I have to. My father and mother mustn't know I'm doing this, and neither must Dan Kalmus."

"Then it's impossible." Wolfe tore pages loose and dropped them on the fire. "Why must they not know?"

"Because they wouldn't let—they'd stop it. I'm sure my father would." She was gripping the bag. "Mr. Wolfe, I came to you because I had to. I knew I'd have to tell you things I shouldn't tell anybody. This is the first good thing I have ever done. That's the trouble with me, I never do anything bad and I never do anything good, so what's the use? And I'm twenty-two years old, that's why I brought twenty-two thousand dollars."

She patted the bag. "But I'm doing this. Dan Kalmus has been my father's lawyer for years, and he may be good at business things, but he's no good for this. I *know* he isn't; I've known him all my life. Last week I told him he should get you, get you to help, and he smiled at me and said no, he didn't like the way you work. He says he knows what he's doing and it will be all right, but it won't. I'm afraid; I'm scared clear through." She leaned forward. "Mr. Wolfe, my father will be convicted of *murder*."

Wolfe grunted. He tore pages. "If your father wants to hire

me I might consider it without his attorney's approval, but it would be difficult."

She was shaking her head. "He wouldn't. If Dan Kalmus said no, he wouldn't. And my mother wouldn't if my father said no. So it's just me. I can hire you, can't I?"

"Certainly not. Without the cooperation of your father and his attorney I couldn't move a finger." Wolfe tore pages with a little extra force. Twenty-two grand wouldn't break any record, but it would be a nice start on 1962.

"That's silly," Miss Blount said. "Of course your mental processes are stultified by the fire. Why I told Dan Kalmus to get you, and why I came, I thought you could do things that nobody else can do. You're supposed to be a wizard. Everyone says you are. Dan Kalmus himself said you're a wizard, but he doesn't want you taking over his case. That's what he said, 'my case.' It's not his case, it's my father's case!"

"Yes," Wolfe agreed, "your father's case, not yours. You must—"

"I'm making it mine! Didn't I say this is the first good thing I've ever done?" Leaning forward, she grabbed his wrist and jerked his hand away from the dictionary, and hung on to the wrist. "Does a wizard only do easy things? What if you're the only man on earth who can save my father from being convicted of a murder he didn't do? If there was something I could do that no one else on earth could do, I'd do it! You don't need my father or his attorney because I can tell you anything they can. I can tell you things they wouldn't, like that Dan Kalmus is in love with my mother. Dan Kalmus wouldn't, and my father couldn't because he doesn't know it, and he's in jail and I'm not!"

She turned loose the wrist, and Wolfe tore out pages and dropped them on the fire. He was scowling, not at the dictionary. She had hit exactly the right note, calling him a wizard and implying (not inferring) that he was the one and only—after mentioning what she had in her bag.

He turned the scowl on her. "You say you know he didn't do it. Is that merely an opinion seemly for a daughter or can you support it with evidence?"

"I haven't any evidence. All the evidence is against him. But it's not just an opinion, I *know* it. I know my father well enough to—"

"No." He snapped it. "That is cogent for you but not for

me. You want to engage me, and pay me, to act on behalf of a man without his knowledge—a man who, in spite of his wealth and standing, has been charged with murder and locked up. The evidence must be strong. Your father wouldn't be my client; you would."

"All right, I will." She opened the bag.

"I said *would*. It's preposterous, but it is also tempting. I need to know—but first what Mr. Goodwin and I already know." His head turned. "Archie. What do we know?"

"The crop?" I asked. "Or the high lights?"

"Everything. Then we'll see if Miss Blount has anything to add."

"Well." I focused on the prospective client. "This is from the papers and some talk I've heard. If I'm wrong on anything don't try to remember until I'm through, stop me. The Gambit Club is a chess club with two floors in an old brick building on West Twelfth Street. It has about sixty members, business and professional men and a couple of bankers. As chess clubs go, it's choosy. Tuesday evening, January thirtieth, two weeks ago tomorrow, it had an affair. A man named Paul Jerin, twenty-six years old, not a member, was to play simultaneous blindfold games with twelve of the members.

"About Paul Jerin. I'm mixing the papers and the talk I've heard without separating them. He was a screwball. He had three sources of income: from writing verses and gags for greeting cards, from doing magic stunts at parties, and from shooting craps. Also he was hot at chess, but he only played chess for fun, no tournament stuff. You knew him. You met him—how long ago?"

"About a year. I met him at a party where he did tricks."

"And he cultivated you—or you cultivated him. I've heard it both ways—of course you realize there's a lot of talk, a thing like this. Learning that he played chess, you arranged for him to play a game with your father, at your home. Then he came again, and again. How often? I've heard different versions."

"He played chess with my father only three times. Three evenings. He said it was no fun because it was too easy. The last time he gave my father odds of a rook and beat him. That was months ago."

"But aside from chess you saw a lot of him. One version, you were going to marry him, but your father—"

"That's not true. I never dreamed of marrying him. And I didn't see a lot of him. The police have asked me about it, and I know exactly. In the last three months I saw him just five times, at parties, mostly dancing. He was a good dancer. No girl with any sense would have *married* him."

I nodded. "So much for talk. But you got your father to arrange that affair at the Gambit Club." We had to keep our voices up because of the noise Wolfe made tearing paper.

"They've asked me about that too," she said. "The way it happened, Paul suggested it to me, he said it would be fun to flatten their noses, and I told my father, but I didn't *get* him to do it. He said he thought two or three of the members could beat Paul with him playing blindfold, and he arranged it."

"Okay, he arranged it. Of course that's important. Did your father know that Paul always drank hot chocolate when he was playing chess?"

"Yes. Paul drank hot chocolate when he was doing almost anything."

"Then we'll tackle the affair of January thirtieth. It was stag. Men only."

"Yes."

"This is from the papers. I read murders in the papers, but with full attention only when we're in on it, so I may slip up. If I do, stop me. No one was there but club members, about forty of them, and Paul Jerin, and the steward, named Bernard Nash, and the cook, named Tony Laghi. In a big room on the ground floor there were twelve chess tables, in two rows, six tables in each row, ranged along the two long walls, and at each table a club member sat with his back to the wall. They were the players. That left room in the middle, the length of the room, for the other members to move around and watch the play. Right?"

"Yes."

"But four of the other members didn't just watch the play, they were messengers. Paul Jerin was in a smaller room to the rear of the house which one paper, I think the *Times*, said contains the best chess library in the country. He was sitting on a couch, and, after play started, he was alone in the room. The tables were designated by numbers, and each messenger served three tables. When play started a messenger went in to Jerin and told him the table—"

"Not when play started. A man playing blindfold has white at all the boards and makes the first move."

"I should think he'd need it. Anyway, whenever a member at one of the tables made a move the messenger serving that table went in to Jerin and told him the table number and the move, and Jerin told him his move in reply, and he went back out to the table and reported it. Right?"

"Yes."

"Okay, but I don't believe it. I have monkeyed with chess a little, enough to get the idea, and I do not believe that any man could carry twelve simultaneous games in his head without seeing the boards. I know men have done it, even twenty games, but I don't believe it."

Wolfe grunted. "One hundred and sixty-nine million, five hundred and eighteen thousand, eight hundred and twenty-nine, followed by twenty-one ciphers. The number of ways the first ten moves, both sides, may be played. A man who can play twelve simultaneous games blindfold is a *lusus naturae*. Merely a freak."

"Is that material?" I asked him.

"No."

I returned to Sally Blount. She had told me on the phone that her name was Sarah but everyone called her Sally and she preferred it. "Play was to start at eight-thirty," I said, "but it actually started at eight-forty, ten minutes late. From then on Jerin was alone in the library except when one of the messengers entered. I think I can name them. Charles W. Yerkes, banker. Daniel Kalmus, attorney-at-law. Ernst Hausman, wealthy retired broker, one of the founders of the club. Morton Farrow, a nephew of Mrs. Matthew Blount, your mother." I paused, shutting my eyes. I opened them. "I pass. I'm sure one of the papers said what your cousin Morton does for a living, but I can't recall it."

"He's in my father's business." Her brows were up, making her eyes even bigger. "You must have a good memory, even without your full attention."

"My memory is so good I'm practically a freak, but we keep newspapers for two weeks and I admit I looked them over after you phoned. From here on you may know things that haven't been published. The police and the District Attorney always save some details. I know from the papers that your father played at Table Number Six. That the steward and the cook, Bernard Nash and Tony Laghi, were in the kitchen in the basement, down a flight. That shortly after play started a pot of hot chocolate was taken from the kitchen to Paul Jerin in the library, and he drank some, I don't know how much, and about half an hour later he told one of the messengers, Yerkes, the banker, that he didn't feel well, and at or about nine-thirty he told another messenger, Kalmus, the lawyer, that he couldn't go on; and Kalmus went and brought a doctor, one of the players—I don't know which table—named Victor Avery. Dr. Avery asked Jerin some questions and sent someone to a drug store on Sixth Avenue for something. By the time the medicine arrived Jerin was worse and the doctor dosed him. In another half an hour Jerin was even worse and they sent for an ambulance. He arrived at St. Vincent's Hospital in the ambulance, accompanied by Dr. Avery, at a quarter to eleven, and he died at twenty minutes past three. Later the Medical Examiner found arsenic in him. The *Times* didn't say how much, but the *Gazette* said seven grains. Any correction?"

"I don't know."

"Not published if the arsenic was in the chocolate. Was it?"

"I don't know."

"Also not published, the name of the person who took the chocolate from the kitchen up to the library. Do you know that?"

"Yes. My father did."

I gawked at her. Wolfe's hand stopped short on its way to the fire with pages. I spoke. "But your father was at Table Six, playing chess. Wasn't he?"

"Yes. But when he made his second move the messenger for that table, Mr. Hausman, wasn't there at the moment, and he got up and went to see if Paul had been supplied with chocolate. Table Six was at the end of the room next to the library. The chocolate hadn't been brought, and my father went down to the kitchen and got it."

"And took it up to Jerin himself?"

"Yes."

Wolfe shot a glance at her. I took a breath. "Of course I believe you, but how do you know?"

"My father told me. The next day. He wasn't arrested until Saturday—of course you know that. He told my mother and me exactly what happened. That's partly why I know he didn't do it, the way he told us about it, the way he took it for granted that we would know he didn't do it." Her eyes went to Wolfe. "You would say that's not cogent for you, but it certainly is for me. I *know*."

"Okay," I said, "he delivered the chocolate. Putting it on a table by the couch Jerin was sitting on?"

"Yes. A tray, with the pot and a cup and saucer and a napkin."

"You say your father told you all about it. Did Jerin eat or drink anything besides the chocolate?"

"No. There was nothing else."

"Between the time your father took him the chocolate and the time he told Yerkes he didn't feel well, about half an hour, did anyone enter the library besides the messengers?"

"No. At least my father thought not, but he wasn't absolutely certain." She looked at Wolfe. "I can ask him. You said you couldn't move a finger without his cooperation, but I can get to see him and ask him anything you want me to. Of course without telling him it's for you."

No comment. He tore pages out.

I eyed her. "You said you don't know if the arsenic was in the chocolate. Didn't your father mention if there was any left in the pot and if it was kept for the police?"

"Yes, it was kept, but the pot was full."

"Full? Hadn't Jerin drunk any?"

"Yes, he had drunk a lot. When Mr. Yerkes told my father that Paul had told him he wasn't feeling well, my father went to the library. The pot had a little left in it, and the cup was half full. He took them down to the kitchen and rinsed them out. The cook and steward said nothing had been put in but milk and powdered chocolate and sugar. They had some more ready, and they filled the pot, and my father took it up to the library with a clean cup. Apparently Paul didn't drink any of that because the pot was still full."

I was staring at her, speechless. Wolfe wasn't staring, he was glaring. "Miss Blount," he said. "Either your father is an unexampled jackass, or he is innocent."

She nodded. "I know. I said I'd have to tell you things I shouldn't tell anybody. I've already told you Dan Kalmus is in love with my mother, and now this. I don't know whether my father has told the police about it. I suppose the cook and steward have, but maybe they haven't. But I had to tell you, I have to tell you everything I know, so you can decide what to do. Don't I?"

"Yes. I commend you. People seldom tell me everything they know. The cook and steward have of course told the police; no wonder your father has been charged with murder." Wolfe shut his eyes and tried leaning back, but it was no go in that chair. In the made-to-order oversized chair at his desk that was automatic when he wanted to consider something, leaning back and closing his eyes, and, finding that it wouldn't work, he let out a growl. He straightened up and demanded, "You have money in that bag?"

She opened it and took out a fat wad of bills with rubber bands around them. "Twenty-two thousand dollars," she said, and held it out to him.

He didn't take it. "You said you sold some things. What things? Yours?"

"Yes. I had some in my bank account, and I sold some jewelry."

"Your own jewelry?"

"Yes. Of course. How could I sell someone else's?"

"It has been done. Archie. Count it."

I extended a hand and she gave me the wad. As I removed the rubber bands and started counting, Wolfe tore out pages and dropped them on the fire. There wasn't much of the dictionary left, and, while I counted, five-hundreds and then C's, he tore and dropped. I counted it twice to make sure, and when I finished there was no more dictionary except the binding.

"Twenty-two grand," I said.

"Will this burn?" he asked.

"Sure; it's buckram. It may smell a little. You knew you were going to burn it when you bought it. Otherwise you would have ordered leather."

No response. He was bending forward, getting the binding satisfactorily placed. There was still enough fire, since Fritz had used wood as well as kindling. Watching the binding starting to curl, he spoke. "Take Miss Blount to the office and give her a receipt. I'll join you shortly."

2

Twenty-two thousand dollars is not hay. Even after expenses and taxes it would make a healthy contribution to the up-keep of the old brownstone on West Thirty-fifth Street, owned by Wolfe, lived in and worked in by him, by Fritz Brenner, chef and housekeeper, and by me, and worked in by Theodore Horstmann, who spent ten hours a day, and sometimes more, nursing the ten thousand orchids in the plant rooms at the top of the house. I once calculated the outgo per hour for a period of six months, but I won't mention the figure because the District Director of Internal Revenue might read this and tell one of his sniffers to compare it with the income tax report. As for the twenty-two grand, received in cash, he would find it included in income.

But when, at a quarter past one, I returned to the office after letting Sally Blount out and put the wad in the safe, I was by no means chipper. We had the wad with no strings attached; Wolfe had made it clear that his only commitment was to give it a try, but it seemed more than likely that we were licked before we started, and that's hard to take for the ego of a wizard, not to mention a dog.

I had filled a dozen pages of my notebook with such items as: 1. As far as Sally knew, none of the four messengers, the only ones besides her father and the cook and steward who had been in reaching distance of the chocolate, had ever seen Paul Jerin before or had any connection with him; and if they had she would almost certainly have known because they were all in the Blounts' circle, one way or another, and she saw them fairly frequently. Ditto for Bernard Nash and Tony Laghi, the steward and cook, though she had never seen them.

2. The messengers. Charles W. Yerkes, the banker, had occasional social contacts with the Blounts. Blount was on the Board of Directors of Yerkes's bank. Yerkes enjoyed being

in the same room with Mrs. Blount, Sally's mother, but so did lots of men. In my notes I included a parenthesis, a guess that Sally thought it would be just as well if men would take time out from looking at her mother to give her a glance now and then. That was a little odd, since Sally herself was no eyesore, but of course I hadn't seen her mother.

. 3. Morton Farrow, age thirty-one, was not a wizard, but wasn't aware of it. He drew a good salary from the Blount Textile Corporation only because he was Mrs. Blount's nephew, and thought he was underpaid. I'm translating what Sally told us, not quoting it.

4. Ernst Hausman, retired broker, a lifelong friend of Matthew Blount, was Sally's godfather. He was an unhappy man and would die unhappy because he would give ten million dollars to be able to play a chess master without odds and mate him, and there was no hope. He hadn't played a game with Blount for years because he suspected Blount of easing up on him. He had disapproved of the idea of having Paul Jerin come to the club and do his stunt; he thought no one but members should ever be allowed in. In short, a suffering snob.

5. Daniel Kalmus, the lawyer, had for years been counsel for Blount's corporation. Sally had some kind of strong feeling for him, but I wasn't sure what it was, and I'm still not sure, so I'll skip it. She had said that Yerkes was in his forties, and Hausman, her godfather, was over seventy, but she said definitely that Kalmus was fifty-one. If a twenty-two-year-old girl can rattle off the age of a man more than twice as old who is not a relative and with whom she isn't intimate, there's a reason. There were other indications, not only things she said but her tone and manner. I put it down that her not trusting Kalmus—she always said "Dan Kalmus," not "Mr. Kalmus" or just "Kalmus"—that her not trusting him to pull her father out of the hole was only partly because she thought he couldn't. The other part was a suspicion that even if he could, he wouldn't. If Blount were sent to the chair, or even sent up for life, Mrs. Blount might be available. Sally didn't say that, but she mentioned for the third time that Dan Kalmus was in love with her mother. Wolfe asked her, "Is your mother in love with him?" and she said, "Good heavens, no. She's not in love with anyone—except of course my father."

6. So much for the messengers. Of the other items in my notebook I'll report only one, the only one that was material.

If any container that had held arsenic had been found the newspapers didn't know about it, but that's the kind of detail the police and DA often save. When Wolfe asked Sally if she knew anything about it I held my breath. I wouldn't have been surprised if she had said yes, a bottle half full of arsenic trioxide had been found in her father's pocket. Why not? But she said that as far as she knew no container had been found. Dr. Avery, who was usually called on by her father or mother when a doctor was needed, had told her father two or three days after the affair, before Blount had been arrested, that after questioning and examining Jerin he had considered the possibility of poison and had looked around; he had even gone down to the kitchen; and he had found nothing. And four days ago, last Thursday, when Sally, after two sleepless nights, had gone to his office to get a pre-scription for a sedative, he had said that he had been told by an assistant DA that no container had ever been found, and now that Blount had been charged and was in custody he doubted if the police would try very hard to find one. The police hadn't been called in until after Jerin died, and Blount, who had walked to the hospital, only a couple of blocks from the Gambit Club, after the ambulance had taken Jerin, had had plenty of opportunity to ditch a small object if he had one he wanted to get rid of. Dr. Avery, convinced that his friend and patient Matthew Blount was innocent, had told Sally that someone must have had a container and disposed of it, and had advised her to tell Kalmus to hire a detective to try to find it. It was that advice from Dr. Avery that had given Sally the idea of coming to Nero Wolfe.

One item not in the notebook. At the end Wolfe told her that it was absurd to suppose that he could act without the knowledge of Kalmus and her father. He would have to see people. At the very least he would have to see the four men who had been messengers, and, since he never left the house on business, they would have to come to him, and Sally would have to bring them or send them. Inevitably Kalmus would hear about it and would tell Blount. Sally didn't like that. For a couple of minutes it had looked as if there was going to be an exchange, me handing her the wad and her giving me back the receipt, but after chewing on her lip for twenty seconds she decided to stick. She asked Wolfe who he wanted to see first, and he said we would let

her know. She asked when, and he said he had no idea, he
had to consider it.

At a quarter past one, when I returned to the office, not
chipper, after letting her out, and put the wad in the safe, he
was sitting straight, his mouth pressed so tight he had no
lips, his palms flat on the desk pad, scowling at the door to
the front room. It could have been either his farewell to the
subversive dictionary or his greeting to a hopeless job,
and it wouldn't help matters any to ask him which. As I
swung the safe door shut, Fritz appeared to announce
lunch, saw Wolfe's pose and expression, looked at me, found
my face no better, said, "All right, you tell him," and went.

Of course business was out at the table, but Wolfe refuses
to let anything whatever spoil a meal if the food is good,
as it always is in that house, and he managed to pretend
that life was sweet and the goose hung high. But when we
finished the coffee, got up, and crossed the hall back to the
office, he went to his desk, sat, rested fists on the chair arms,
and demanded, "Did he do it?"

I raised a brow. If Sally herself had been suspected of
murder I would have humored him, since I am supposed,
by him, after an hour or so in the company of an attractive
young woman, to be able to answer any question he wants
to ask about her. But it was stretching it too far to assume
that my insight extended to relatives I had never seen, even
a father.

"Well," I said. "I admit that if there is anything to the
idea of guilt by association there can also be innocence by
association, but I recall that you once remarked to Lewis
Hewitt that the transference—"

"Shut up!"

"Yes, sir."

"Why didn't you intervene? Why didn't you stop me?"

"My job is starting you, not stopping you."

"Pfui. Why in heaven's name did I consent? The money?
Confound it, I'll take to a cave and eat roots and berries.
Money!"

"Nuts are good too, and the bark of some trees, and for
meat you could try bats. It was only partly the money. She
said you can do things no one else on earth can do, so when
it developed that prying Blount loose is obviously something
that no one on earth can do you were stuck. Whether Blount
did it or not is beside the point. You have to prove he

didn't even if he did. Marvelous. By far your best case."

"Yours too. Ours. You didn't stop me." He reached to put a finger on the button and pressed it, two short and one long, the beer signal. That was bad. He never rings for beer until an hour after lunch, giving him half an hour or so before he is to leave for his four-to-six afternoon session with Theodore in the plant rooms. I went to my desk. Seated there, my back is to the door to the hall, but in the mirror before me I saw Fritz enter with the beer and stop two paces in to aim his eyes at me with a question in them. One of my two million functions, as Fritz knows, is to keep Wolfe from breaking his beer rules. So I swiveled and said, "Okay. He's taking to a cave, and I'm going along. This is a farewell fling."

Fritz stood. "That woman? Or the dictionary?"

"I don't want the beer," Wolfe said. "Take it back."

Fritz turned and went. Wolfe took in a bushel of air through his nose as far down as it would go, and let it out through his mouth. "I agree," he said. "Consideration of his guilt or innocence would be futile. Either we proceed on the assumption that he is innocent or we withdraw. Do you wish to get that stuff from the safe and go and return it to her?"

"No. We took it and let her go. You know damn well why I didn't try to stop you. It was too good to pass up—the chance of seeing you tackle one that was absolutely impossible."

"You're prepared to assume that Mr. Blount is innocent?"

"Hell, I have to. As you say."

"Then someone else is guilty. I begin by eliminating the cook and the steward."

"Good. That simplifies it. Why?"

"Look at it. The arsenic was in the chocolate. Therefore if either—"

"No. Not known. The only arsenic found was inside Jerin. The pot was full of fresh chocolate, no arsenic, the cup was clean, and no container was found. Not known."

"But it is." Usually Wolfe's tone had a trace of satisfaction when he corrected me, but that time he didn't bother. "After four days of investigation the District Attorney charged Mr. Blount with murder. Blount couldn't possibly have given Jerin arsenic in any medium other than the chocolate. Before arresting him, the possibility that the arsenic had been administered in some other medium had to be eliminated beyond question, and at that sort of inquiry the police are highly competent. Certainly they have established that Jerin didn't swallow the arsenic before he arrived at the Gambit Club, and at the club he swallowed only the chocolate; otherwise they wouldn't have charged Blount."

"Check," I conceded. "The cook and steward?"

"This is not conclusive, only strongly probable. There they were in the kitchen, preparing the chocolate. One or both of them knew Mr. Jerin, had reason to wish him dead, knew he was coming to the club, and knew the chocolate was for him. Confine it to one. He puts arsenic in the chocolate. At the time he does so he doesn't know that Mr. Blount will come for it; he supposes that it will be taken to the library by himself or his colleague. He doesn't know that later Mr. Blount will bring the pot and cup down and rinse them out. He doesn't know that any club member has an animus toward Mr. Jerin—unless you think I should allow that?"

"No."

"He doesn't know if there will be an opportunity for any-one else to put something in the chocolate. He does know that the police will certainly discover his connection, what-ever it is, with Jerin. But he puts arsenic in the chocolate?"

"No. At least we can save them for the last. Of course the cops have checked on them. With Blount and the cook and steward out, what you have left is the messengers. Unless someone sneaked in uninvited?"

He shook his head. "Mr. Blount told his daughter only that he thought not, he wasn't absolutely certain, but his table was near the door to the library. And it would have been foolhardy. Only the messengers were supposed to go in to Mr. Jerin, and anyone else entering would have been observed and noted. It would have been rash beyond sanity. I ex-clude it, tentatively. But there is one other possibility be-sides the messengers, Mr. Jerin himself. He had arsenic in a soluble capsule, put it in his mouth, and washed it down with the chocolate. Shall I deal with that?"

"No, thanks. I don't need help with that one. Deal with the messengers. I grant opportunity. He goes in to report a move, shutting the door. We assume that he shut the door on account of the noise made by the spectators moving around in the big room?"

"Yes."

"Right. He knows that another messenger may enter at any moment, but he only needs five seconds. The pot is there on the table. Jerin, on the couch, has his eyes closed, concentrating. He has the arsenic ready, say in a paper spill, and in it goes. He wouldn't have to stir it. Nothing to it. Shall I name him?"

"Yes indeed."

"Ernst Hausman, the chess fiend. He had been against inviting Jerin to come, but since he was there, there was his chance at a guy who could give odds of a rook to Blount, who could beat *him*. He would have liked to poison all the chess masters alive, beginning with the world champion, who I understand is a Russian."

"Botvinnik."

"Not only a *lusus naturae*, but also a Commie. I know of no case on record where that was the motive, killing a man because he played chess too well, but everything has to have a first. I am not blathering. Hausman may be off the rails."

Wolfe grunted. "Not may be. Is. If he would give a fortune to excel at chess. Then you dismiss the other three."

"I file them. Until I take a look at Hausman. The client says they had never seen Jerin, though they may have heard of him, from her. Of course we might cut a motive to fit the lawyer, Dan Kalmus. He's not really in love with her mother, he's in love with her. Being a married man, if he is, he has to hide his passion for a virgin, if she is, so when he's with the Blounts he ogles the mother as a cover. He has the impression that Sally has fallen for Paul Jerin, which could be true in spite of what she told you, and the thought of her holding hands with another man is unbearable, so he buys some arsenic."

"That's a little farfetched."

"Murder is usually farfetched. Would we settle for making Blount merely an accessory? We have to assume he didn't commit the murder, sure, but he could have suspected that Hausman or Kalmus had doctored the chocolate, so he took care of the pot and cup."

"No." Wolfe shook his head. "Our assumption is that Mr. Blount is not involved. He took the pot and cup, and emptied and cleaned them, because he thought that Jerin's indisposition might have been caused by something in the chocolate— as indeed it had been. A natural and proper action." He

closed his eyes, but he didn't lean back, so he wasn't thinking, he was merely suffering. His lips twitched. After a dozen
or so twitches he opened his eyes and spoke. "At least we
have a free field. The police and District Attorney have
Mr. Blount in custody and are committed; they have no interest in our targets except as witnesses, and of course they
have signed statements from them. There will be no jos-
tling." He looked up at the wall clock. "Mr. Cohen is in his
office?"

"Sure."

"See him. Besides the published accounts we have information from only one source, Miss Blount, and we have no
knowledge of either her competence or her veracity. Tell
Mr. Cohen that I have engaged to inquire into certain aspects of this matter, and I need—"

"It'll be tough—I mean for him. He'll know that can mean
only one thing, that you've been hired to get Blount out, and
you think it can be done or you wouldn't have taken the job,
and to expect him to sit on *that*—I don't know."

"I don't expect him to sit on it."

"He can print it?"

"Certainly. As I told Miss Blount, my intervention can't
be kept secret, and the sooner the murderer knows of it the
better. He may think it necessary to do something."

"Yeah. Of course if—no. I'll have to tie a string on my
finger to remind me that Blount didn't do it." I got up. "If
I don't tell Lon who hired you he'll assume it was Blount.
Kalmus."

"Let him. You can't prescribe his assumptions."

"I wouldn't try. Any particular point or points?"

"No. *All* points."

I went to the hall, got my hat and coat from the rack, let
myself out, and nearly got pushed off the stoop by a gust of
the icy winter wind.

3

In his own little room on the twentieth floor of the *Gazette* building, which had LON COHEN on the door but no title, two doors down the hall from the corner office of the publisher, Lon cradled the phone, one of three on his desk, turned to me, and said, "You may be in time for the twilight if it's a quickie. Front page?"

I slumped and crossed my legs, showing that there was plenty of time. I shook my head. "Not even the second section. I'm just looking for scraps that may not be fit to print. About Paul Jerin and the Gambit Club."

"You don't say." He ran a palm over his hair, which was almost black and slicked back and up over his sloping dome. I knew that gesture well, but had learned the hard way not to try to interpret it. He was next to the best of the poker players I spent one night a week with, the best being Saul Panzer, whom you will meet later on. He asked, "Doing research for a treatise on adult delinquency?"

"All I would need for that would be a mirror. Nero Wolfe is inquiring into certain aspects of the matter."

"Well well. Just for curiosity?"

"No. He has a client."

"The hell he has. For release when?"

"Oh, tomorrow."

"Who's the client?"

"I don't know. He won't tell me."

"I'll bet he won't." Lon leaned forward. "Now look, Archie. It's basic. In a newspaper sentences must always be active, never passive. You can't say 'Mr. Kaczynski was bitten by a woman today.' You must say 'Miss Mabel Flum bit Mr. Kaczynski today.' The lead-off on this must be, 'Daniel Kalmus, attorney for Matthew Blount, has engaged Nero Wolfe to get evidence that Blount did not murder Paul Jerin.' Then further along mention the fact that Wolfe is the greatest

19

detective this side of outer space and has never failed to deliver, with the invaluable assistance of the incomparable Archie Goodwin. That's the way to do it."

I was grinning at him. "I like it. Then the next day you could feature Kalmus's denial."

"Are you saying it's not Kalmus?"

"I'm not saying. What the hell, it's just as good, even better, leaving it open who hired him, hinting that you know but you're not telling. Next day they'll buy a million *Gazettes* to find out."

"Are you going to fill it in any? Now?"

"No. Not a word. Just that he's been hired and has been paid a retainer."

"Can we say we have it direct from you?"

"Sure."

He turned and got at a phone, the green one. It didn't take long, since he only had enough for one short paragraph. He hung up and turned to me. "Just in time. Now for tomorrow's follow-up. I don't expect words and music, but what's the slant that makes Wolfe think—"

"Whoa." I showed him a palm. "You've got the gall of a journalist. It's my turn. I want everything about everybody that you know or guess but haven't printed."

"That would take all night. First, off the record, does Wolfe actually expect to spring Blount?"

"Off the record, that's the idea." I had my notebook out. "Now. Have they found a container with arsenic in it?"

"I'll be damned." His head was cocked. "Does Wolfe know that Blount went down to the kitchen for the chocolate and took it up to Jerin?"

"Yes."

"Does he know that after Jerin had drunk most of the chocolate Blount took the cup and pot away and rinsed them out?"

"Yes."

"Does he know that Blount chased Jerin out of his apartment and told him to stay away from his daughter?"

"No. Do you?"

"I couldn't prove it, but the word is that the cops can. And one of our men got it—a good man, Al Proctor—he got it from a friend of Jerin's. Do you want to talk to Proctor?"

"No. What for? That would only help on a motive for

Blount, and since Blount's innocent why waste time on it? Have they—"

"I *will* be damned. My God, Archie, this is hot! Come on, give! Off the record until you say the word. Have I ever fudged on you?"

"No, and you won't now. Skip it, Lon. Nothing doing. Have they found a container?"

He reached for a phone, sat a moment with his fingers on it, vetoed it, and settled back. "No," he said, "I don't think so. If they had I think one of our men would know."

"Did Jerin know or suspect he had been poisoned?"

"I don't know."

"*Gazette* men must have talked with men who were there."

"Sure, but the last four hours, at the hospital, only doctors and nurses were with him and they don't talk."

"At the club, Jerin didn't point to someone and say, 'You did this, you bastard'?"

"No. If he had, whom should he have pointed to?"

"I'll tell you later. Not today. Who went to the hospital? I know Dr. Avery went in the ambulance, and Blount went. Who else?"

"Three of the club members. One of them was Kalmus, the lawyer. I can get the names of the other two if you want them."

"Not unless it was Hausman or Yerkes or Farrow."

"It wasn't."

"Then don't bother. What's the talk in the trade? I've heard this and that, at the Flamingo and around, but I don't see much of journalists except you. What are they saying? Have they got angles?"

"None that you would like. Of course there were plenty of angles the first few days, but not since they took Blount. Now the big question is did Jerin lay Sally or didn't he. That wouldn't interest you."

"Not a particle. Then they all think Blount's wrapped up? No minority opinion?"

"None worth mentioning. That's why this from you, and Wolfe, is a bomb. Now there *will* be angles."

"Fine. So there's been no interest in anyone else since Blount was charged, but how about before that? The four

messengers. Hausman, Yerkes, Farrow, Kalmus. You must
have got quite a collection of facts you didn't print."

He eyed me exactly the way he eyed me when I took
another look at my hole card, lifted one brow, and raised
him the limit. "I'd give more than a nickel," he said, "I'd
give a shiny new dime, to know which one of them you want
to know about. Damn it, we could help. We have our share of
beetle-brains, but also there's a couple of good men. At
your service."

"Wonderful," I said. "Send me their names and phone
numbers. Tell them not to call me, I'll call them. Now tell
me about the messengers. Start with Kalmus."

He told me. Not only what he had in his head; he sent
for the files. I filled eight pages of my notebook with the most
useless-looking conglomeration of facts you could imagine.
Of course you never know; Wolfe had once been able to
crack a very hard nut only because Fred Durkin had
reported that a certain boy had bought bubble gum at two
different places, but there's no point in bothering to tell you
that Yerkes had been a halfback at Yale or that Farrow had
a habit of getting bounced out of night clubs. I'll keep it to a
minimum:

Ernst Hausman, seventy-two, retired but still owner of a
half interest in a big Wall Street firm, was a widower with no
children, no friends (Blount didn't count?), and no dogs. His
obsession with chess was common knowledge. Owned the
finest collection of chessmen in the world, some two hundred
sets, one of Imperial jade, white and green.

Morton Farrow, thirty-one, single, lived at the Blount
apartment on Fifth Avenue (not mentioned by Sally). He
was an assistant vice-president of the Blount Textiles Corporation. Had got a ticket for speeding the night of January
thirtieth, the night of the affair at the Gambit Club.

Charles W. Yerkes, forty-four, senior vice-president of the
Continental Bank and Trust Company, was married and had
two children. At the age of twenty-six he had come out
eleventh in a field of fourteen in the annual tournament for
the United States chess championship, and had entered no
tournament since.

Daniel Kalmus, fifty-one, prominent corporation lawyer, a
partner in the firm of McKinney, Best, Kalmus, and Green,
was a widower, with four children, all married. One of the
club members had told a *Gazette* reporter that he had

been surprised that Kalmus had been a messenger instead of playing, because he thought that Kalmus, the club's best player, could have beaten Jerin.

And so forth. While I was going through the files Lon made a couple of phone calls and received a couple, but he kept me in a corner of his eye. Presumably the idea was that if Wolfe was particularly interested in one of that quartet I might show it by a flicker of the eye or a twist of the lip. Not wanting to disappoint him, I eased a slip of paper out and slipped it up my cuff, and later, when I put the folders back on his desk, he asked, "Would you like a copy of the item in your sleeve?"

"All right, I tried," I said, and fingered it out and forked it over. All it had on it, scribbled in pencil, was *2/8 11:40 A.M. LC says MJN says too much chess AR.* I said, "If LC means Lon Cohen that may settle it."

"Go climb a tree." He dropped it in the wastebasket. "Anything else?"

"A few little details. What's Sally Blount like?"

"I thought Blount was out of it."

"He is, but she may have some facts we need, and it'll help to know what to expect when I see her. Is she a man-eater?"

"No. Of course she's still an angle with us, and presumably with the cops. With most girls of her age and class you'll find a little dirt, sometimes a lot, if you dig, but apparently not with her. She seems to be clean, which should be newsworthy but isn't. We have nothing on her, even with Paul Jerin, and I doubt if the cops have."

"College?"

"Bennington. Graduated last year."

"How about her mother? Of course she's not an angle, but she may have some facts too. Know anything about her?"

"I sure do. I've told my wife that she needn't wonder what I'll do if she dies. I'll get Anna Blount. I don't know how, but I'll get her."

"So you know her?"

"I've never met her, but I've seen her a few times, and once is enough. Don't ask me why. It's not just looks or the call of the glands. She's probably a witch and doesn't know it. If she knew it it would show, and that would spoil it. As you say, she's not an angle, but, with her husband arrested for murder, she's news, and it appears that I'm not the only one. She attracts. She pulls."

"And?"

"Apparently there is no and. Apparently she's clean too. It's hard to believe, but I'd like to believe it. As you know, I'm happily married, and my wife is healthy, and I hope she lives forever, but it's nice to know that such a one as Anna Blount is around just in case. I can't understand why I don't dream about her. What the hell, a man's dreams are private. If you see her be sure to tell me how you take it."

"Glad to." I rose. "I'm not thanking you this time because I gave more than I got."

"I want more. Damn it, Archie, just a little something for tomorrow?"

I told him he would get more if and when there was more, got my coat and hat from the other chair, and went.

I walked downtown. That would have been ideal for arranging my mind, my legs working, my lungs taking in plenty of good cold air, and a few snowflakes coming at me and then away from me, if there had been anything in my mind to arrange. Even worse, my mind was refusing to cooperate on the main point. I had bought the assumption that Matthew Blount was innocent, but my mind hadn't. It kept trying to call my attention to the known facts, which was subversive.

Headed south on Sixth Avenue, my watch said 4:30 as I approached Thirty-fifth Street, and instead of turning I continued downtown. Wolfe wouldn't come down from the plant rooms until six o'clock, and there was no point in going home just to sit at my desk and try to get my mind on something useful when there was nothing useful to get it on. So I kept going, clear to Twelfth Street, turned left, stopped half way down the long block, and focused on a four-story brick building, painted gray with green trim, across the street. A brass plate to the right of the door, nice and shiny, said GAMBIT CLUB. I crossed the street, entered the vestibule, tried the door, but it was locked, pushed the button, got a click, opened the door, and entered.

Of course I was just kidding my mind. There wasn't a chance in a million that I would get any new facts for it to switch to, but at least I could show it that I was in charge. There was a long rack in the hall, and, as I disposed of my coat and hat, a man appeared in an open doorway on the right and said, "Yes, sir?"

It was Bernard Nash, the steward. There had been a pic-

ture of him in the *Gazette*. He was tall and narrow with a
long sad face. I said, "I'm checking something," and made
for the doorway, but without giving me room to pass he
asked, "Are you from the police?"

"No," I said, "I'm a gorilla. How often do you have to see
a face?"

He would probably have asked to see my buzzer if I
hadn't kept moving, and I brushed against him as I went
through. It was the big room. Evidently the chess tables had
been specially placed for the affair, for there were now
more than a dozen—more like two dozen—and three of them
were in use, with a couple of kibitzers at one. Halting only
for a quick glance around, I headed for an open door at the
rear end, followed by the steward. If Table Six, Blount's, had
been in the row at the left wall, he had been sitting only
ten feet from the door to the library.

The library was almost small enough to be called cozy,
with four leather chairs, each with a reading light and a
stand with an ashtray. Book shelves lined two walls and part
of a third. In a corner was a chess table with a marble top,
with yellow and brown marble for the squares, and the men
spread around, not on their home squares. The *Gazette* had
said that the men were of ivory and Kokcha lapis lazuli and
they and the table had belonged to and been played with
by Louis XIV, and that the men were kept in the position
after the ninth move of Paul Morphy's most famous game,
his defeat of the Duke of Brunswick and Count Isouard in
Paris in 1858.

The couch was backed up to the left wall, but there was
no table, just stands at the ends. I looked at Nash. "You've
moved the table."

"Certainly." Since I was just a cop, so he thought, no "sir"
was required. "We were told things could be moved."

"Yeah, the inspector would, with members in the high
brackets. If it had been a dump he'd have kept it sealed for
a month. Has your watch got a second hand?"

He glanced at his wrist. "Yes."

"All right, time me. I'm checking. I'm going down to the
kitchen and coming right back. I'll time it too, but two
watches are better than one. When I say 'go.'" I looked at
my watch. "Go." I moved.

There were only two doors besides the one we had entered by, and one of them was to the hall, and near the

other one, at the far end, was a little door that had to be to an old-fashioned dumb-waiter shaft. Crossing to it—not the dumb-waiter—I opened it and stepped through. There was a small landing and stairs down, narrow and steep. Descending, I was in the kitchen, larger than you would expect, and nothing old-fashioned about it. Stainless steel and fluorescent lights. A round little bald guy in a white apron, perched on a stool with a magazine, squinted at me and muttered, "My God, another one."

"We keep the best till the last." I was brusque. "You're Laghi?"

"Call me Tony. Why not?"

"I don't know you well enough." I turned and mounted the stairs. In the library, Nash, who apparently hadn't moved, looked at his watch and said, "One minute and eighteen seconds."

I nodded. "Close enough. You said in your statement that when Blount went down the first time to get the chocolate he was in the kitchen about six minutes."

"That's wrong. I said about three minutes. If you don't— Oh. You're trying to— I see. I know what I said in my statement."

"Good. So do I." I went to the door to the big room, on through, and to the table where the game had a couple of kibitzers. Neither they nor the players gave me a glance as I arrived. More than half of the men were still on the board. One of Black's knights was attacked by a pawn, and I raised a brow when he picked up a rook to move it, but then I saw that the white pawn was pinned. Nash's voice came from behind my shoulder. "This man is a police officer, Mr. Carruthers." No eyes came to me, not an eye. White, evidently Mr. Carruthers, said without moving his head, "Don't interrupt, Nash. You know better."

A fascinating game if it fascinates you. With nothing better to do, I stuck with it for half an hour, deciding for both White and Black what the next move should be, and made a perfect record. Wrong every time. When Black moved a rook to where a knight could take it, but with a discovered check by a bishop which I hadn't seen, I conceded I would never be a Botvinnik or even a Paul Jerin and went to the hall for my hat and coat. The only words that had passed had been when White had pushed a pawn and Black had murmured, "I thought you would," and White had murmured, "Obvious."

It was snowing harder, but there were still twenty minutes before six o'clock, so I walked some more. As for my mind, I told it that it now had some new data to work on, since I had shown it the scene of the crime and had even established the vital fact that it took seventy-eight seconds to go down to the kitchen and back up, but it wasn't interested. Around Eighteenth Street I gave up and began to look at people going by. Girls are better looking in snowstorms, especially at night.

When I mounted the stoop of the old brownstone and used my key I found that the bolt wasn't on, so I didn't have to push the button for Fritz. Shaking the snow off my coat and hat before entering, putting them on the hall rack, and proceeding to the office, the only greeting I got was a sidewise glance. Wolfe was at his desk with his current book, *African Genesis*, by Robert Ardrey. Crossing to my desk, I sat and picked up the late edition of the *Gazette*. We have three copies delivered, one for Wolfe, one for Fritz, and one for me. It was on the front page, the first item under LATE BULLETINS.

Wolfe must have been on a long paragraph, for a full minute passed before he looked up and spoke.

"It's snowing?"

"Yes. And blowing some."

His eyes went back to his book. "I hate to interrupt," I said, "but I might forget to mention it later. I saw Lon Cohen. He got it in today, as you may have noticed."

"I haven't looked. Did you get anything useful?"

"Not useful to me. Possibly to you." I got my notebook from my pocket.

"Doubtful. You have a nose." He went back to his book.

I gave him time for another paragraph. "Also I went and had a look at the Gambit Club."

No comment.

"I know," I said, "that that book is extremely interesting. As you told me at lunch, it tells what happened in Africa a hundred thousand years ago, and I realize that that is more important than what is happening here now. My talk with Lon can wait, and all I did at the Gambit Club, besides taking a look at the couch Jerin sat on, was watch a game of

chess, but you told Miss Blount you would let her know who
you want to see first. If you expect her to get someone here
this evening I ought to phone her now."

He grunted. "It isn't urgent. It's snowing."

"Yeah. It may clear up by the time the trial starts. Don't
you think?"

"Confound it, don't badger me!"

So he was phutzing. Since one of my most important
functions is needling him when his aversion to work takes
control, it was up to me, but the trouble was my mind.
Showing it the scene of the crime had accomplished nothing. If I couldn't sick it onto the job how could I expect to
sick him? I got up and went to the kitchen to ask Fritz if
there had been any phone calls, though I knew there hadn't,
since there had been no note on my desk.

However, there were three calls in the next hour, before
dinner, and two during dinner—the *Times*, the *Daily News*,
and the *Post*, and two of the networks, CBS and NBC. With
all of them I confirmed the item in the *Gazette* and told them
we had nothing to add. The *News* was sore because I had
given it to the *Gazette*, and of course the *Times* tried to insist
on speaking with Wolfe. When the last trumpet sounds the
Times will want to check with Gabriel himself, and for the
next edition will try to get it confirmed by even Higher
Authority.

I had returned to the dining room after dealing with CBS,
to deal with my second helping of papaya custard, when the
doorbell rang. During meals Fritz answers it. He came from
the kitchen, went down the hall to the front, and in a minute
came back, entered, and said, "Mr. Ernst Hausman. He said
you would know the name."

Wolfe looked at me, not as at a friend or even a trusted
assistant. "Archie. This is your doing."

I swallowed custard. "No, sir. Yours. The *Gazette*. I merely followed instructions. You said the murderer might think
it necessary to do something, and here he is."

"Pfui. Through a blizzard?"

He really meant it. On a fine day he would venture out to
risk his life in the traffic only on a strictly personal errand,
and this was night and snow was falling. "He had to," I said.
"With you on it he knew he was done for and he came to
confess." I pushed my chair back and left it. A man coming

without an appointment before we had had our coffee—he was capable of telling Fritz to tell him to come tomorrow morning.

"Okay, Fritz," I said, "I'll do it."

4

We always have our after-dinner coffee in the office, mainly because the chair behind his desk is the only one that Wolfe can get his bulk really comfortable in, and of course the guest had to be invited to partake. He said he'd try it, he was very particular about coffee, and when Fritz put a cup on the stand by the red leather chair and was going to pour he said the cup was too small and told Fritz to bring a larger one. Ideal company. He must have been fun at dinner parties.

He didn't look his seventy-two years, and I had to admit he didn't look like a murderer, but murderers seldom do. One thing was sure, if he murdered at all he would use poison, because with a gun or knife or club he might get spots on his perfectly tailored three-hundred-dollar suit or his sixty-dollar shoes or his twenty-dollar tie, or soil his elegant little hands, or even spatter blood on his neat little face with its carefully barbered mustache.

He lifted the larger cup and took a sip. "Quite good," he conceded. He had a thin finicky voice. He took another sip. "Quite good." He looked around. "Good room. For a man in your line of work quite unexpected. That globe over there—I noticed it when I came in. What's its diameter? Three feet?"

"Thirty-two and three-eighths inches."

"The finest globe I ever saw. I'll give you a hundred dollars for it."

"I paid five hundred."

Hausman shook his head and sipped coffee. "Not worth it. Do you play chess?"

"Not now. I have played."

"How good were you?"

Wolfe put his cup down. "Mr. Hausman. Surely you didn't come through a snowstorm at night for this." He reached for the pot.

"Hardly." He showed his teeth. It wasn't a grin; it was simply that his lips suddenly parted enough for his teeth to show and then closed again. "But before I go into matters I have to be satisfied about you. I know you have a reputation, but that doesn't mean anything. How far can you be trusted?"

"That depends." Wolfe put the pot down. "I trust myself implicitly. Anyone else will do well to make certain of our understanding."

Hausman nodded. "That's always essential. But I mean —uh—suppose I hire you to do a job, how far can I depend on you?"

"If I commit myself, to the extent of my abilities. But this is fatuous. Do you hope to determine my quality by asking banal and offensive questions? You must know that a man can have only one invulnerable loyalty, loyalty to his own concept of the obligations of manhood. All other loyalties are merely deputies of that one."

"Hunh," Hausman said. "I'd like to play you a game of chess."

"Very well. I have no board or men. Pawn to Queen Four."

"Pawn to Queen Four."

"Pawn to Queen Bishop Four."

"Pawn to King Three."

"Knight to King Bishop Three."

"You mean Queen Bishop Three."

"No. King Bishop Three."

"But the Queen's Knight is a better move! All the books say so."

"That's why I didn't make it. I knew you would expect it and know the best answer to it."

Hausman's lips worked a little. "Then I can't go on. Not without a board." He picked up his cup, emptied it, and put it down. "You're sharp, aren't you?"

"I prefer 'adroit,' but yes."

"I have a job for you." He showed his teeth. "Who has hired you to work on that—uh—murder at the Gambit Club? Kalmus?"

"Ask him."

"I'm asking you."

"Mr. Hausman." Wolfe was patient. "First you inquired about my furniture and my habits, then about my probity, and now about my private affairs. Can't you contrive a question which deserves an answer?"

"You won't tell me who hired you?"

"Of course not."

"But someone did?"

"Yes."

"Then it must have been Kalmus. Or Anna—Mrs. Blount . . ." He took a moment to consider it. "No. Kalmus. He has had no experience with this kind of thing and no talent for it. I am Matthew Blount's oldest friend. I knew him as a boy. I am his daughter's godfather. So I am interested, deeply interested, in his—uh—welfare. And with Kalmus handling this there's no hope for him, no hope at all. Kalmus has hired you, but you're under his direction and control, and with him in charge there's no hope. He has paid you a retainer. How much?"

Wolfe's shoulders went up an eighth of an inch and down again. He looked at me with his brows raised, saying without words, "See what you let in?"

"Then you won't," Hausman said. "All right, that can wait. I want to hire you to do something that will get results. There will be no conflict of interest because this is in Matthew Blount's interest too. I'll pay you myself. I may get it back from Blount later, but that's no concern of yours. How much do you already know about what happened that night at the Gambit Club?"

"Enough, perhaps. If I lack needed information you can probably supply it."

"You know about the chocolate? That the police theory is that Blount poisoned that man by putting arsenic in the chocolate?"

"Yes."

"Then all we have to do is to prove that somebody else put arsenic in the chocolate. That would free Blount?"

"Yes."

"Then that's the thing to do. I thought of this last week, but I knew how Kalmus would react if I went to him with it, and I didn't want to do it myself because there are certain —uh—difficulties. Then today I saw that item in the paper about you. I asked you how far I can count on you because this has to be absolutely confidential. Would you do something that would free Blount without telling Kalmus, before or after?"

"If it were something I had engaged to do, yes."

"And without telling anyone else?"

"If I had made the engagement with that condition, yes."

"It will be with that condition." Hausman looked at me. "What's your name?"

"Archie Goodwin."

"Leave the room."

I put my coffee cup down. I seldom drink three cups, but the situation had got on my nerves hours ago, and that bozo wasn't helping any. "Anything to oblige a client," I said, "but you're not a client yet. If I left, I'd have to stand at the peephole to look and listen, and I'd rather sit."

He looked at Wolfe. "This is for you only."

"Then it's not for me. What's for me is categorically for Mr. Goodwin."

I thought for ten seconds Hausman was going to call it off, and so did he. He showed his teeth, and his lips stayed parted for a full ten seconds while his eyes went back and forth to Wolfe and me. Finally they settled on Wolfe, and he spoke. "I act on impulse. I came here on impulse. You said something about a man's loyalty to his concept of the obligations of manhood, and I owe this to Matthew Blount. I'm a hard man, Wolfe. If you or Goodwin cross me you'll regret it."

Wolfe grunted. "Then we must be at pains not to."

"You had better. No man has ever crossed me without regretting it. I want you to get proof that someone else put the arsenic in the chocolate. I'll tell you exactly how to do it. All you have to do is follow instructions. I have it planned to the last detail."

"Indeed." Wolfe leaned back. "Then it shouldn't be difficult. You say 'someone.' Any particular one?"

"Yes. His name is Bernard Nash. He's the steward of the Gambit Club. There was arsenic there in the kitchen. Isn't arsenic used to poison rats?"

"It has been. It can be."

"There was some there in the kitchen, and by mistake Nash put some in the chocolate. Perhaps instead of sugar. When I said I have it planned to the last detail I meant the basic details. You will arrange the minor details with Nash, of course without any mention of me—the kind of container the arsenic was in, where it was kept, how much he put in the chocolate—all such points. Also, of course, how and when he disposed of the container afterward. When Blount went down to the kitchen with the pot and cup and emptied them —do you know about that?"

"Yes."

"He told the steward and the cook that Jerin was ill and asked about the chocolate. After he left, with the fresh chocolate, Nash thought about it, and realized what he had done, and disposed of the container with arsenic in it. Isn't that plausible?"

"It's credible."

"Of course that will have to be carefully considered—how and where and when he disposed of the container. I realize that in a matter like this nothing can be overlooked, absolutely nothing. That's why I came to you. With your experience, you know exactly what the police will do. You will know how to arrange it so there will be no possibility of a slip. But on one point I'm going to insist. Nash will have to retract what he has told the police—undoubtedly he has signed a statement—and he must have a good reason. The reason will be that after Kalmus hired you, you saw Nash and questioned him, and you forced him to admit what he had done. I insist on that. That way there will be no indication that I have had a hand in it. Of course you agree."

Wolfe was rubbing his nose with a finger tip. "I might, after talking with Mr. Nash. Has he agreed?"

"Certainly not. But he will, with the inducement you'll offer. That won't be the difficulty, getting him to do it; the difficulty will be arranging all the little details so the police will be satisfied. That's up to you."

"What inducement will I offer?"

"That's up to you too. I'll pay you fifty thousand dollars, and you'll give me a receipt for payment in full for services rendered. I think if you offer Nash half that amount, twenty-five thousand, that will be ample. He has personal difficulties and needs money badly. Only a month ago he appealed to me for help. He wanted me to lend him fifteen thousand dollars, but I would never have got it back. His wife is ill and needs a series of operations and other expensive treatment, he's in debt on account of her, and he has two sons in college, and two daughters. He has the stupid pride of a man who can't afford pride. All you're asking him to do is admit he made a mistake. A mistake isn't a crime. With twenty-five thousand dollars he could get a good lawyer, and with a good lawyer he would probably get off. Wouldn't he?"

Wolfe flipped a hand. "That would be his risk, not yours or mine. To our risk we could not plead inadvertence. It's barely possible that I misunderstand you, and, as I said, we should be certain of our understanding. Have you any evidence that Mr. Nash did in fact put arsenic in the chocolate?"

"No."

"Or any reason to suppose that he did?"

"Reason." Hausman showed his teeth. "Reason? No."

"Then our risk would be formidable. If Mr. Nash accepted the offer and collaborated with me on contrivance of the details, naturally I would put them in an affidavit for him to sign. Without such an affidavit we would have nothing. And if he repudiated it later, we would have no defense to a charge of subornation of perjury. No lawyer could get *us* off. We would—"

"Not us. You. Your share of the—"

"Pfui." Wolfe had straightened up. "Mr. Hausman. I do not say that I would suborn perjury in no conceivable circumstances. But if I did so for money, and if it became known, do you imagine I would refuse to disclose who had paid me? Or that Mr. Goodwin would refuse to confirm it? To show his appreciation for our cooperation, the judge might in his mercy sentence us to five years instead of six. Or even four."

"It would be two against one, but a man of my standing—"

"Bah. Asked what you paid me fifty thousand dollars for, what would you say?" Wolfe shook his head. "You said that you know my reputation but it doesn't mean anything. Assuredly it doesn't to you, since, knowing it, you come to me with this witless proposal. Why? You're not a nincompoop. It invites conjecture. Are you concerned not for Mr. Blount, but for yourself? Did you put the arsenic in the chocolate, and does Mr. Nash know it or suspect it, and is this your devious—"

The phone rang. I swiveled and got it. "Nero Wolfe's residence, Archie Goodwin speaking."

"Mr. Goodwin, this is Sally Blount. I want to speak with Nero Wolfe."

"Hold the wire." I covered the receiver and turned. "That girl who came this morning about her jewelry."

He was frowning because he had had a speech interrupted. "What does she want?"

"You."

He tightened his lips, turned and glared at his phone, then reached for it. I put mine to my ear. "Yes, madam? This is Nero Wolfe."

"This is Sally Blount, Mr. Wolfe."

"Yes."

"I know you never go anywhere, but you have to. You *must*. You must come and talk with my mother. You didn't say you were going to put it in the paper."

"I didn't decide to until after you left. Your name wasn't mentioned."

"I know, but when my mother saw it she guessed. She didn't guess, she *knew*. She knew I had tried to persuade Dan Kalmus, and I had tried to persuade her too—didn't I tell you that?"

"No."

"I should have. Well, she knew, and I had to admit it, and you'll have to come and talk with her. Right away. *Now*."

"No. Bring her here tomorrow morning."

"It has to be *now*. She has phoned Dan Kalmus, and he may come, and . . . you *must!*"

"No. Out of the question. But if you apprehend—you are at home?"

"Yes."

"Mr. Goodwin will go. Shortly."

"It ought to be you! Surely you can—"

"No. Mr. Goodwin will be there within half an hour."

He hung up, but, since I was on, the line was still open and she was talking. I cut in. "Save it. Relax. Expect me in twenty minutes." I cradled the phone and left my chair. Wolfe had pushed the button, and, as I headed for the hall, Fritz appeared at the door.

"Come, Fritz," Wolfe said. "Take Archie's chair. Your memory may not match his, but it will serve."

"Yes, sir." As Fritz moved he winked at me, and as I passed him I winked back.

5

In the marble lobby of the marble tenement on Fifth Avenue in the Seventies, I was expected. The man in uniform didn't even let me finish. When I said, "Name, Archie Goodwin, to see—", he broke in, "Yes, Mr. Goodwin," and showed me to the elevator. But he phoned while I was being lifted, for when I emerged on the sixteenth floor the client was there, standing in the doorway. She put a hand out, not as an offer to shake but asking for help. I took it with my right and gave it a pat with my left as I told her, "Nineteen minutes. Taxi drivers don't like snow."

Inside, in a foyer the size of Wolfe's office, after I had shed my hat and coat she led me through an arch and across a dozen yards of rug to a fireplace. On the way I took a glance around. Pictures, chairs, a piano in a corner, doodads on stands, potted plants on a rack that took up most of the far end, lamps here and there. The fireplace, where a fire was going, was three times as wide as the one Wolfe used for burning dictionaries.

"Sit down," Sally said. "I'll bring my mother, but I don't know what you're going to say to her. Do you?"

"Of course not. It depends. What's the pinch?"

"She says I must call it off—with Nero Wolfe. She's going to tell Dan Kalmus to tell my father, and I know what he'll say. I'm *sure* he will." She put finger tips on my arm. "I'm going to call you Archie."

"Good. I answer to it."

"I can't call him Nero, I don't think anybody could, but I can call you Archie, and I'm going to. This morning, did I say this is the first good thing I have ever done?"

"Yes."

"Well, it is, and I'm doing it, but I have to know somebody is with me. Really *with* me." Her fingers were around my arm. "Will you? Are you? Archie?"

36

My mind wasn't. It was still with the facts. But having it put to me straight like that, if I had tried hedging I wouldn't have been loyal to my concept of the obligations of manhood. It had to be either yes or no. "Okay," I said, "since it's the first good thing you've ever done I'm with you all the way. Anyhow, you're Nero Wolfe's client and I work for him, so everything fits. As for what I'll say to your mother, I'll decide that when I see her. If she's willing to—"

I stopped because her eyes left me. With her back to the fireplace, she had the room in view and I didn't. I turned. A woman had entered and was approaching. Sally spoke. "I was coming for you, mother. Mr. Wolfe couldn't come. This is Archie Goodwin."

I would have appreciated better light. The lamps were shaded and not close. As she came near the firelight played on her face, but that's tricky; one second she looked younger than her daughter, and the next, she was a hag. "You'll forgive me if I don't shake hands, Mr. Goodwin," she said. "I wouldn't mean it. Please sit down."

She didn't sit, she sank, into an armchair on the right. I took one at right angles to her and twisted to face her. Sally stood. I spoke. "Your daughter asked me what I was going to say to you, and I told her I didn't know. She has hired Nero Wolfe to do a job for her and I work for him. If I tell you anything about it, it will have to be with your daughter's consent. She's the client."

Her eyes were brown like Sally's, but not as big. "You're a private detective," she said.

"Right."

"It's grotesque." She shook her head. "A private detective telling me my daughter is his client and he can talk to me only with her consent. But of course it's all grotesque. My husband in jail charged with murder. He has a lawyer, a good one. My daughter can't hire a private detective without his approval. I have told her that, and now you must tell her. That's . . . isn't that wrong? It must be."

Taking her in, I was making allowances. When lots of men had enjoyed being in the same room with her (according to Sally), and when Lon Cohen had been bewitched by her on sight, the circumstances had been different. The strain of the past ten days had to be considered, and allowing for it, I conceded that I too might have enjoyed being in the same room with her. I suspected that she might even

have what will pull three men out of five, that without
knowing it she could give you the feeling that she knew absolutely nothing but understood everything. It's a rare gift.
I once knew a woman in her sixties who—but Mrs. Blount
had asked me a question. She had a long way to go to her
sixties.

"That depends," I said. "If your daughter's over twenty-
one and she pays Mr. Wolfe with her own money, who can
say it's wrong?"

"I can. I'm her mother."

I nodded. "Sure, but that doesn't settle it, that just starts
an argument. If by 'wrong' you mean illegal or unethical, the
answer is no. Isn't it fairly simple, Mrs. Blount? Isn't it just
a difference of opinion? Your daughter thinks the services of
Nero Wolfe are needed, and you don't. Isn't that it?"

"No. I mean it's not just a difference of opinion."

"Then what is it?"

Her lips parted and closed again. Her eyes went to Sally
and came back to me. "I don't know what my daughter has
told you," she said.

I turned to Sally. "This isn't going to get us anywhere
unless I have a free hand. Unless you turn me loose, no
strings. Yes or no?"

"Yes," she said.

"I'm not a wizard, Sally."

"That's all right if you meant what you said about being
with me."

"I did. Sit down."

"I'd rather stand."

I turned to Mrs. Blount. "Your daughter told Mr. Wolfe
that her father thinks Dan Kalmus is competent to handle
his defense, and you do too, but she doesn't; that Kalmus
may be good on business matters but he is no good for this;
and she is afraid that if it is left to Kalmus her father will
be convicted of murder. So I still say it's a difference of
opinion. Admitting that she may be wrong, it's her opinion,
and it's her money. And even if she's wrong and Kalmus
makes good, why all the fuss? She'll have the satisfaction of
making a try, her father will be free, and Mr. Wolfe will
collect a fee, so everyone will be happy. The only ground
for objection is that Mr. Wolfe might mess it up and make it
tougher instead of easier, and of course for him and me

that's out. It would also be out for anyone who knows his record."

She was slowly shaking her head, and I, looking at her, was getting a faint glimmer of the impression she had made on Lon Cohen. It didn't come from her eyes or from anything about her you could name, it simply came somehow from her to me, the idea that though she could explain nothing, she didn't have to; between her and me no explanation was needed. Of course that can come to a man from any woman he has fallen for, or is falling, but I wasn't falling for her, far from it, and yet I was distinctly feeling it. Probably a witch and didn't know it, Lon had said. A damned dangerous woman, whether she knew it or not.

She spoke. "It's not that, Mr. Goodwin."

Guessing what a woman means is usually the shortest way, but guessing that one wrong would have been risky, so I asked, "What's not what, Mrs. Blount?"

"Read this," she said, and extended a hand with a folded paper.

I took it and unfolded it. It was memo size, 4 × 6, good quality, with *from the desk of Daniel Kalmus* printed at the top. Written on it with a ball-point pen was this:

Friday.

My dearest—I send this by Dan. Tell Sally I know she means well, but I fully agree with Dan about her idea of hiring that detective, Nero Wolfe. I don't see how it could help and it isn't necessary. As Dan has told you, there is a certain fact known only to him and me which he will use at the right time and in the right way—a fact I haven't told even you. Don't worry, my dearest, don't worry, and tell Sally not to—Dan knows what he's doing. All my love,

Your Matt

I read it twice, folded it, and handed it back to her. "I still say it's a difference of opinion. Of course you have shown that to your daughter?"

"Yes."

"Have you any idea what the fact is, the fact that your husband says is known only to him and Kalmus?"

"No."

I turned. "Have you, Sally?"

"No," she said.

"Not even a wild guess?"

"No."

"You see why this is wrong," Mrs. Blount said. "Mr. Kalmus has spoken with me on the phone, and he says that item in the paper has already done harm because everyone will think he has hired Nero Wolfe. So tomorrow the paper must say that it was a mistake, that no one has hired Nero Wolfe. Whatever my daughter has paid him, that doesn't matter, he can keep it."

I looked up at Sally, who was still standing. My mind, still harping on the facts, of course excluding the one known only to Kalmus and Blount, wanted to grab at the excuse to ditch the whole damn mess. If Kalmus already had a fact that would do the trick, that was that; and if he didn't, the chance that there was one somewhere and Wolfe and I could dig it up looked slimmer than ever. Of course we would have to return the twenty-two grand. Whenever Wolfe sent me on an errand without specific instructions the general instruction was that I was to use my intelligence guided by experience. I would have to go home and tell him that I had done so and had concluded that we should drop it. So I looked up at Sally. If she had been looking at me with any sign of doubt or funk I might have passed. But she had her big brown eyes aimed straight at her mother, no blinking, with her chin up and her lips tight. So I turned to Mrs. Blount and said, "All right, I admit it's not just a difference of opinion."

She nodded. "I was sure you would understand if I showed you that note from my husband."

I shook my head. "That's beside the point. The point is that your daughter has paid Mr. Wolfe twenty-two thousand dollars, and in order to—"

"I said he could keep it."

"He only keeps money he earns. In order to get that amount she cleaned out her bank account and sold her jewelry. A girl doesn't sell her jewelry just like that." I snapped my fingers. "I'm not telling you now what she told Mr. Wolfe, I'm telling you what I inferred from what she did tell him. She told him three times that Kalmus is in love with you. I inferred that she thinks her father will be convicted of murder not just because Kalmus is incompetent, but because with Blount convicted and sent up either to the chair or for life, you would be loose. So if that's what—"

"Stop," she said. She was sitting straight, stiff, staring at me, frowning. "I'm not sure I understand. Are you saying that Mr. Kalmus *wants* my husband to be convicted?"

"No. I'm saying that I believe your daughter thinks he does. So she sold her jewelry. And she certainly deserves—"

"Stop." She was on her feet. She moved, across to her daughter, and gripped her arms. "Sally," she said, "my dear Sally. You can't think . . . you *can't!*"

"Yes I can," Sally said. "I do. You know he's in love with you. You know he would do anything, *anything*, to have you. Are you blind, mother? Are you *blind*? Do you actually not see how men look at you? How Dan Kalmus always looks at you? I was going . . . last week I was going to—"

A voice came booming, "Anybody home?"

I turned. A man had passed through the arch and was coming. Mrs. Blount said, raising her voice, "We're busy, Mort," but, not stopping, he said, "Maybe I can help," and, arriving, kissed her on both cheeks. Sally had backed away. He turned for a look at me, started to say something, stopped, and looked some more. "You're Archie Goodwin," he said. "I've seen you around." He offered a hand. "I'm Mort Farrow. You may have seen me too, but I'm not a famous detective so I don't get pointed out." He wheeled to his aunt. "I had that dinner date, but I broke away as soon as I could. I thought something might be stirring when I heard about Nero Wolfe. Was it you, or Dan? Or Uncle Matt? Brief me, huh?"

A fine moment for a six-foot big-mouth to break in. If I had been his aunt or uncle and he had been living under my roof I would have trimmed him down to size long ago. But Anna Blount only said, no protest, "It was a mistake, Mort —about Nero Wolfe. I was explaining to Mr. Goodwin. I'll tell you about it later." Her eyes came to me. "So you see, Mr. Goodwin, it was just a—a mistake. A misunderstanding. I'm sorry, we regret it very much, and Mr. Kalmus will tell the newspaper. As for the money, please tell Nero Wolfe—"

She stopped, sending her eyes past me, and I turned. There had been a sound of a gong off somewhere, and through the arch I caught a glimpse of a maid's uniform passing in the foyer. In a moment a man's voice came, and in another moment the man appeared. He halted to dart a glance around, then came on, and Mrs. Blount took three steps to meet him. As he took her hand he said something so low I didn't catch it, and she said, "Mr. Wolfe didn't come, but Mr. Goodwin is here and I've been explaining to him." I hadn't sat down again after rising to shake with Morton Farrow, and so was on my feet when the newcomer, nodding to Sally and Farrow, faced me, extended a hand, and said, "I'm Dan Kalmus. In a case one of my partners tried a couple of years ago he had to cross-examine you and he hasn't forgotten it."

I might or might not have known him from the picture the *Gazette* had had. In the flesh he didn't have much flesh, just bones and skin—felt on his hand and seen on his jaw and cheeks. With no wrinkles or creases and his full share of hair with no gray, he didn't look the fifty-one years Sally had given him.

"I'm afraid I have," I said. "So he must have made a monkey of me."

"He did not. On the contrary." He was squinting at me. "Mrs. Blount says she has explained the situation to you, but can I add anything? Do you want to ask me anything?"

"Yes. What's the fact that is known only to you and Mr. Blount?"

His eyes widened for a second, then squinted again. "You know," he said, "that might be a good question if Wolfe were on the case. But since he isn't, since Mrs. Blount has explained, it's out of order. You know?"

I decided to pass the buck to Sally, since it really depended on her. If she hung on with Kalmus present, after the fur I had started flying, that would settle it for good as far as I was concerned. "That would be a good answer," I said, "if Mr. Wolfe were out of the case. But as far as I know, he isn't. Let's ask Miss Blount, she hired him." I turned to her. "What about it? Do you want out?"

"No." It came out a croak, and she repeated it. "No."

"Do you want Mr. Wolfe to go on with it? And me?"

"Yes."

"Then I have a sugges—"

"Now come off it, Sally." Kalmus had turned to face her. "You stubborn little imp. If your dad were here—anyway he is, by proxy." He tapped his chest. "Me. It's an order, from him, by him, and for him. You can't disobey an order from your dad."

"Yes I can." She had drawn back when he stepped close. "I would even if he were here and told me himself. He trusts you and I don't."

"Nonsense. You're not qualified to judge my professional competence. You don't even—"

"It's not just your professional competence. I don't *trust* you. Tell him, Archie."

I told his back, "Miss Blount considers that if her father is convicted and sentenced you can make a set at his wife, and she thinks that that may be affecting your judgment. It was on account of that—"

He had whirled and pulled a fist back, his right, and was starting it for my face. Anna Blount made a grab for his arm and missed. The nephew took a step and stopped. I could have ducked and jabbed him in the kidney, but he was so slow it was simpler to sidestep and get his wrist as it came and give it a good twist. It hurt, but the damn fool started his left, and I jerked him around and as he went down to his knees I sent my eyes to Farrow, who had taken another step.

"I wouldn't," I said. "I'm probably in better condition and I've had more practice." I looked at Kalmus, who was scrambling up. "If you must hit somebody hit Miss Blount. I was merely telling you what she thinks. That's why she came to Nero Wolfe, and that's why she won't let go." I turned to her. "I was saying, I have a suggestion. It's not going to be very pleasant for you here. If you'd like to spend the night with some friend, and if you want to pack a bag, I'll be glad to take you. I'll wait downstairs. Of course if you prefer to stay here and take it—"

"No." She moved. "I'll pack a bag." She headed for the arch, and I followed. From behind, Mrs. Blount said something, but we kept going. In the foyer she said, "I won't be long. You'll wait?" I said I would, took my hat and coat, let myself out, and pushed the elevator button.

I put it at fifty-fifty, an even chance that either her mother or Kalmus, or both, would talk her out of leaving, and down in the lobby I considered alternatives. My watch said 10:41. I would give her half an hour, and then I would go back up, or I would go to a phone booth on Madison Avenue and ring her, or I would go home, report to Wolfe, and let him use *his* intelligence guided by experience. But she saved me the trouble of deciding. I had just looked at my watch and seen 10:53 when the elevator door closed, and in a couple of minutes it opened again, and there she was, in the pallid mink, with a matching turban, and luggage—not just an overnight bag, a medium-size brown leather suitcase.

Her face was glum but grim, with her jaw set. The hallman was coming for the suitcase, but I was there first. I asked him to get a taxi, and when he was outside I asked her if she had phoned someone, and she said no, she hadn't decided where to go. She was going on, but the hallman got a break on a snowy night. A cab pulled up at the curb outside, and I ushered her out, let the flunky put the luggage in with the driver, handed him a quarter, got in after the client, told the hackie the first stop would be the nearest phone booth, and we rolled. Sally started to say something, but I put a finger to my lips and shook my head. The hackie might not only know the address of Matthew Blount who was booked for murder, he might even have recognized his daughter from her picture in the paper, and there was no point in letting him in on the latest development. He turned right on Seventy-eighth Street, right again on Madison, and in a couple of blocks stopped in front of a drugstore.

I leaned forward to poke a dollar bill at him. "Here," I said, "go in and blow it. Aspirin, cigarettes, lipstick for your wife, whatever you need. We're going in conference. I'll come in for you, say ten minutes, maybe less."

"Can't," he said. "The law."

"Nuts. If a cop shows I'll tell him it's an emergency." I got out my card case and showed him my license. He gave it a look, said, "Oh. How-do-you-do," took the dollar, climbed out, and went.

Sally gave me her face. "I'm glad you did that," she blurted. "I'm *glad*."

"Sure," I said, "I thought we could use a little privacy. Taxi drivers talk too much. Now if you've decided—"

"I don't mean that. I mean I'm glad you told my mother. And him. I wanted to, but I couldn't. Now they know. How did you know?"

"The deductive process. I'm a licensed detective, so I'm allowed to guess. Have you decided where you're going?"

"Yes, I'm going to a hotel—some little hotel. You know about hotels, don't you?"

"Yeah. But . . . haven't you any friends with an extra bed?"

"Of course I have. I was going to phone one, but then I

thought what would I say? All of a sudden like this, eleven o'clock at night . . . I'd have to give some reason, and what could I say? With all the talk . . ." She shook her head. "I'm going to a hotel."

"Well." I gave it a look. "That might be even worse. You could use another name, but if someone spots you and the papers get onto it, talk about talk. Good headlines. BLOUNT'S DAUGHTER FLEES HOME IN MIDDLE OF NIGHT. Also possibly that I escorted you. The hallman. I showed the cab driver my license."

"Oh. That would be awful." She eyed me. Silence. My hand was there on the seat between us, and she touched it. "It was your suggestion," she said.

"Ouch," I said. "But so it was. Okay. As you may know, I live where I work, in Nero Wolfe's house. There's a room above his on the third floor which we call the south room. It has a good bed, two windows, its own bath, hot and cold running water, a Kashan rug fifteen by eleven, and a bolt on the door. The best cook in New York, Fritz Brenner, would get your breakfast, which you could eat either from a tray in your room or in the kitchen with me. His sour milk griddlecakes are beyond any—"

"But I couldn't," she blurted. "I might have to stay . . . I don't know how long . . ."

"It's cheaper by the month. We'll take it out of the twenty-two grand. Anyway, you couldn't pay a hotel bill, you've even sold your jewelry. Of course you'll never live it down, shacking up with three unmarried men, and one of them a Frenchman, but you can't sleep in the park."

"You're making a joke of it, Archie. It's no joke."

"The hell it isn't. That a girl wearing a ten-thousand-dollar coat, with her own bed in a sixteen-room Fifth Avenue apartment, with a flock of friends so-called, with credit in any hotel in town, needs a safe place to sleep? Certainly it's a joke."

She tried to smile and nearly made it. "All right," she said. "Some day maybe I can laugh at it. All right."

I got out and headed for the drugstore to get the hackie.

6

At a quarter past nine Tuesday morning, seated with Sally at the side table in the kitchen, I passed her the guava butter for her third griddlecake. I had told her the household morning routine when I had taken her and the suitcase up to the south room an hour after midnight—Wolfe, breakfast in his room at 8:15 from a tray taken up by Fritz, and to the plant rooms at nine o'clock for two hours with the orchids; and me, breakfast in the kitchen whenever I got down for it, no set time, and then, unless there was an outside errand, to the office for dusting, putting fresh water in the vase on Wolfe's desk, opening the mail, finishing with the morning *Times* if I hadn't done so at breakfast, and performing whatever chores were called for.

Wolfe had done pretty well, for him. He had been at his desk with *African Genesis* when I had entered with Sally at eleven-thirty, and at least he hadn't got up and marched out when I announced that we had a house guest. After a growl and a couple of deep breaths he had put his book down, and when I asked if he wanted just a summary or the whole crop, verbatim, he said verbatim. It's more satisfactory to report a lot of conversation in the presence of someone who was in on it, just as a kid named Archie, years ago out in Ohio, got a bigger kick climbing to the top of a tree if a girl was there watching. Or fifteen or twenty girls. When I was through and he had asked a few questions, he told the client about the caller we had had earlier in the evening, Ernst Hausman, her godfather—not verbatim, but the gist of it. The end of that was for me too, since the phone call from Sally had come just as Wolfe was conjecturing that Hausman had put the arsenic in the chocolate himself. He had not broken down and confessed. After a few rude remarks he had got up and gone.

Wolfe had had no instructions and no comments before going up to bed.

The *Times* had a two-inch paragraph on page twenty-seven, saying that Archie Goodwin had told a *Times* reporter that Nero Wolfe had been retained in connection with the Jerin murder case, but that Daniel Kalmus, Matthew Blount's attorney, had stated that he had not engaged Wolfe's services and he doubted if anyone had.

At breakfast Sally and I had decided a) that it was desirable for her mother to know where she was, b) that she would phone to tell her, c) that she would go out and around at will but would be in her room at eleven o'clock, in case Wolfe wanted her when he came down from the plant rooms, d) that she would help herself to any of the books on the shelves in the office except *African Genesis*, e) that she would not go along when I walked to the bank to deposit the twenty-two grand, and f) that she would join us in the dining room for lunch at 1:15.

I was at my desk at eleven o'clock when the sound came of the elevator, which Wolfe always uses and I never do. He entered, with the day's desk orchids as usual, said good morning, went and put the branch of Laelia gouldiana in the vase, sat, glanced through the morning mail, focused on me, and demanded, "Where is she?"

I swiveled. "In her room. Breakfast with me in the kitchen. Good table manners. She phoned her mother to tell her where she is, went to Eighth Avenue to buy facial tissues because she doesn't like the brand we have, returned, and took three books from the shelves with my permission. I have been to the bank."

He left his chair and went across to the shelves for a look. I doubt if he really could tell, from the vacant spaces among the twelve hundred or so books, which ones she had taken, but I wouldn't have bet on it either way. He went back to his desk, sat, narrowed his eyes at me, and spoke. "Not another coup for you. Not this time."

"Maybe not," I conceded. "But when Mrs. Blount said you could keep whatever her daughter had paid you it looked ticklish, so I spilled it. Or do you mean my telling Kalmus?"

"Neither one. I mean your bringing her here. You did it, of course, to press me. Pfui. Knowing I would sooner have a tiger in my house than a woman, you thought I would—"

"No, sir. Not guilty." I was emphatic. "I start pressing, or trying to, only when you're soldiering, and you've had this

only twenty-four hours. I brought her because if she went
to a hotel there was no telling what might happen. She might
cave in. She might even lam. I told Mrs. Blount you only
keep money you earn. It would be embarrassing not to have
the client available to return the fee to when you decide
you can't earn it. I admit you have stirred up some dust by
having me toss it to Lon Cohen, you even got an offer of
fifty grand from maybe the murderer, but what next? Hope
for a better offer from one of the others?"

He made a face. "I'll speak with Miss Blount after lunch.
I must first see them—Mr. Yerkes, Mr. Farrow, Dr. Avery,
and, if possible, Mr. Kalmus. It may not be—"

"Avery wasn't a messenger."

"But he was at the hospital with Jerin until he died. He
told Mr. Blount that even at the Gambit Club he had considered the possibility of poison and looked around; he had
gone down to the kitchen. If there is any hope of getting—"

The doorbell rang. I rose and went to the hall for a look
through the one-way glass panel in the front door, stepped
back into the office, and said, "More dust. Cramer."

He grunted. "Why? He has *his* murderer."

"Yeah. Maybe for Miss Blount. To take her as an accessory."

"Pah. Bring him."

Going to the front, I took a couple of seconds to observe
him through the one-way glass before opening the door. With
Inspector Cramer of Homicide West there are signs I am
familiar with—the set of his broad burly shoulders, the red-
ness of his big round face, the angle of his old felt hat.
When it's obvious, as it often is, that he intends to dingdong,
I open the door a crack and say something with a point to
it, such as, "A man's house is his castle." But that time he
looked fairly human, so I swung the door wide and greeted
him without prejudice, and, entering, he let me take his
coat and hat, and even made a remark about the weather
before proceeding to the office. You might have thought we
had signed up for peaceful coexistence. In the office, of
course he didn't offer Wolfe a hand, since he knows how he
feels about shaking, but, as he lowered his big fanny onto
the red leather chair, he said, "I suppose I should have
phoned, but you're always here. I wish to God I could always be somewhere. What I want to ask, the Jerin case.

Matthew Blount. According to the papers, you've been hired to work on it. According to Goodwin."

"Yes," Wolfe said.

"But according to Blount's attorney you *haven't* been hired. Who's right?"

"Possibly both of us." Wolfe turned a palm up. "Mr. Cramer. There are alternatives. Mr. Kalmus has hired me but prefers not to avow it, or Mr. Blount has hired me independently of his attorney, or someone else has hired me. In any case, I have been hired."

"By whom?"

"By someone with a legitimate interest."

"Who?"

"No."

"You're working on it?"

"Yes."

"You refuse to tell me who hired you?"

"Yes. That has no bearing on your performance of your duty or the demands of justice."

Cramer got a cigar from a pocket, rolled it between his palms, and stuck it in his mouth. Since he never lights one, the palm-rolling is irrelevant and immaterial. He looked at me, went back to Wolfe, and said, "I think I know you as well as anybody does, except maybe Goodwin. I don't believe Kalmus would hire you and then say he hadn't. What possible reason could he have to deny it? I don't believe Blount would hire you without his lawyer's approval. What the hell, if it was like that he'd get another lawyer. As for someone else, who? The wife or daughter or nephew wouldn't unless Blount and Kalmus approved, and neither would anyone else. I don't believe it. Nobody has hired you."

A corner of Wolfe's mouth was up. "Then why bother to pay me a call?"

"Because I know you. Because you may be on to something. You had Goodwin pass that to his friend Lon Cohen, that you had been hired, to start something that would result in your *being* hired and getting a fee. I don't know what you expected to start, I don't know why you played it like that instead of going to Kalmus with it, whatever you've got, but the point is that you've got something or you wouldn't have played it at all. You've got something that you think will get you a fat fee, and the only way to get a fat fee would be to spring Blount. So what have you got?"

Wolfe's brows were up. "You actually believe that, don't you?"

"You're damn right I do. I think you know something that you think will get Blount out, or at least that there's a good chance. Understand me, I don't object to your copping a fee. But if there's any reason to think Blount didn't murder Paul Jerin I want to know it. We got the evidence that put him in, and if there's anything wrong with it I have a *right* to know it. Do you have any kind of an idea that I would like to see an innocent man take a murder rap?"

"That you would like to, no."

"Well, I wouldn't." Cramer pointed the cigar at Wolfe and waggled it. "I'll be frank. Do you know that Blount went down to the kitchen for the chocolate and took it up to Jerin?"

"Yes."

"Do you know that when Jerin drank most of it and got sick Blount went and got the pot and cup and took them down to the kitchen and rinsed them out, and got fresh chocolate and took it up?"

"Yes."

"Then is he the biggest goddam fool on earth?"

"I haven't met him. Is he?"

"No. He's a very intelligent man. He's anything but a fool. And he's level-headed. Some men fixed like him, men of wealth and standing, have the idea that they can do anything they please, and get away with it, because they're above suspicion, but not him. He's not like that, not at all. So I took it easy—or rather, I didn't. It was hard to believe that such a man had put poison in the chocolate and took it to Jerin and then went and got the cup and pot and rinsed them out. I don't have to spell that out."

"No."

"So we covered it good, every angle. We eliminated the possibility that the arsenic had been in something else, not in the chocolate, and I mean eliminated. We established that no one besides Blount and those four men, the messengers, had entered that room, the library, after the chess games started, and the games had been going for about seven minutes when Blount went to see about the chocolate—and I mean established. So that left it absolutely that the arsenic had been put in the chocolate by one of seven men: the four messengers, the cook, the steward, and Blount. Okay. Which one of them, or which ones, had some kind of connection with Jerin? I put eleven of my men on that angle, and the District Attorney put eight from the Homicide Bureau. For that kind of job there are no better men anywhere. You know that."

"They're competent," Wolfe conceded.

"They're better than competent. We got Blount's connection right away, from Blount himself. Of course you know about that. The daughter."

"Yes."

"But we kept the nineteen men on the other six. In four days and nights they didn't get a smell. Even after the District Attorney decided it had to be Blount and charged him, I kept nine of my men on the others. A full week. Okay. You know how it is with negatives, you can't nail it down, but I'll bet a year's pay to one of the flowers in that vase that none of those six men had ever met Paul Jerin or had any connection with him or his."

"I won't risk the flower," Wolfe said.

"You won't?"

"No."

"Then do you think one of them happened to have arsenic with him and put it in the chocolate just because he didn't like the way Jerin played chess?"

"No."

"Then what kind of a game are *you* playing? What can you possibly have that makes you think you can spring Blount?"

"I haven't said I have anything."

"Nuts. Damn it, I *know* you!"

Wolfe cleared his throat. "Mr. Cramer. I admit that I know something you don't know about one aspect of this matter: I know who hired me and why. You have concluded that no one has hired me, that, having somehow learned of a circumstance not known to you, I am arranging to use it for my private gain. You're wrong; you are incomparably better acquainted than I am with all the circumstances— *all* of them—surrounding the death of Paul Jerin. But you don't believe me."

"I do not."

"Then there's nothing more to say. I'm sorry I have nothing for you because you have put me in your debt. You have just furnished me with a fact which suggests an entirely different approach to the problem. It will save me—"

"What fact?"

Wolfe shook his head. "No, sir. You wouldn't believe me. You wouldn't accept my interpretation of it. But I'm obliged to you, and I don't forget an obligation. If and when I learn something significant I'll stretch a point to share it with you as soon as may be. At present I have nothing to share."

"Like hell you haven't." Cramer got to his feet. He threw the cigar at my wastebasket, twelve feet away, and missed as usual. "One little point, Wolfe. Anyone has a right to hire you to investigate something, even a homicide. But if you haven't been hired, and I know damn well you haven't, if you're horning in on your own, that's different. And if you are in possession of information the law is entitled to—I don't have to tell *you*." He turned and marched out.

I got up and went to the hall, decided he wouldn't properly appreciate help with his coat, and stood and watched until he was out and the door was closed. Turning back to the office, I started, "So he gave you . . . ," and stopped. Wolfe was leaning back with his eyes shut and his lips pushed out. He drew the lips in, then out again, in and out, in and out. I stood and regarded him. That is supposed to be a sign that he's hard at work, but I hadn't the dimmest idea what he was working on. If it was the fact Cramer had just furnished, which one? Running over them in my mind, I stood and waited. The lip exercise is not to be interrupted. I had decided it was going to take a while and was starting for my desk when he opened his eyes, straightened up, and issued a command: "Bring Miss Blount."

I obeyed. As I said, I don't use the elevator; I took the stairs, two flights. Finding the door of the south room closed, I knocked. I heard no footsteps, but in a moment the door opened. There had been no footsteps because she had no shoes on. "Mr. Wolfe wants you," I said. "With or without shoes, as you prefer."

"Has anything happened?"

Not knowing if he wanted her to know we had had a caller, I said, "He just did lip exercises, but of course you don't know how important that is. Don't bother with your lips and hair, he wouldn't know the difference."

Of course that was ignored. She went to the dresser to

use comb and lipstick, then to the chair near a window to put on her shoes, and then came. You get a new angle on a figure when it precedes you down stairs; she had nice shoulders, and her neck curved into them with a good line. As we entered the office Wolfe was frowning at a corner of his desk, rubbing his nose with a finger tip, and we got no attention from him. Sally went to the red leather chair and, after sitting in silence for a full minute, said, "Good morning."

He moved the frown to her, blinked, and demanded, "Why did you take a volume of Voltaire?"

Her eyes widened. "Archie said I could take any book except the one you're reading."

"But why Voltaire?"

"No special reason. Just that I've never read him . . ."

"Unh," Wolfe said. "We'll discuss it at lunch. There has been a development. Did Archie tell—" He stopped short. He had thoughtlessly allowed himself to speak familiarly to a woman. He corrected it. "Did Mr. Goodwin tell you that a policeman has been here? Inspector Cramer?"

"No."

"He has. Uninvited and unexpected. He just left. Mr. Goodwin can tell you later why he came and what was said. What I must tell you, he gave me some information that changes the situation substantially. The police have established, for Mr. Cramer beyond question, three facts. One, that the arsenic was in the chocolate. Two, that no one had an opportunity to put it in the chocolate besides the cook, the steward, the four messengers, and your father. Three, that only your father could have had a motive. None of the other six—I quote Mr. Cramer—'had ever met Paul Jerin or had any connection with him or his.' Though all—"

"I told you that. Didn't I?"

"Yes, but based only on your knowledge, which was deficient. Mr. Cramer's conclusions are based on a thorough and prolonged inquiry by an army of trained men. Though all three of those facts are important, the significant one is the third, that none of those six could have had a motive to kill Jerin. But Jerin was killed—with premeditation, since the arsenic was in hand. Do you play chess?"

"Not really. I know the moves. Do you mean you—"

"If you please. Do you know what a gambit is?"

"Why . . . vaguely . . ."

"It's an opening in which a player gives up a pawn or a piece to gain an advantage. The murder of Paul Jerin was a gambit. Jerin was the pawn or piece. The advantage the murderer gained was that your father was placed in mortal peril—a charge of murder and probable conviction. He had no animus for Jerin. Jerin wasn't the target, he was merely a pawn. The target was your father. You see how that alters the situation, how it affects the job you hired me for."

"I don't . . . I'm not sure . . ."

"You deserve candor, Miss Blount. Till half an hour ago the difficulties seemed all but insurmountable. To take the job and your money I had to assume your father's innocence, but to demonstrate it I had to find evidence that one of those six men had had sufficient motive to kill Jerin and had acted on it. And the three most telling points against your father—that he had taken the chocolate to Jerin, that he had taken the pot and cup and rinsed them, and that he knew Jerin and could plausibly have had a motive—those were merely accidental and had to be ignored. In candor, it seemed hopeless, and, conceiving nothing better for a start, I merely made a gesture; I had Mr. Goodwin arrange for a public notice that I had been hired."

"You didn't tell me you were going to."

"I seldom tell a client what I'm going to do. I tell you now because I need your help. That gesture brought Mr. Cramer, and he brought the fact that it would be fatuous to proceed on the assumption that one of the others had premeditated the murder of Paul Jerin. But, holding to my assumption that your father hadn't, one of the others must have. Why? Jerin was nothing to him, but he went there, with the poison, prepared to kill him, and he did; and what happened? A chain of circumstances pointed so clearly to your father as the culprit that he is in custody without bail, in grave jeopardy. By the operation of cause, calculated cause, and effect. The three most telling points against your father were not accidental; they were essential factors in the calculation. Is that clear?"

"I think . . . yes." She looked at me, and back at Wolfe. "You mean someone killed Paul because he knew they would think my father did it."

"I do. And if it was Mr. Kalmus he also knew he would be in a position, as your father's counsel, to protect his gain from his gambit."

"Yes." Her hands were clenched. "Of course."

"So I propose to proceed on that theory, that Jerin was merely a pawn in a gambit and the true target was your father. If I continue to assume your father's innocence, no other theory is tenable. That gives me a totally new situation, for I now have indications, if the theory is to hold— some facts and some surmises. We'll test them. To avoid verbal complexities I'll call the murderer Kalmus, though I may be slandering him."

He stuck a finger up. "The first fact. Kalmus knew that Jerin would drink or eat something during the game into which arsenic could be put. Preferably, he knew that Jerin would drink chocolate. Did he?"

Sally was frowning. "I don't know. He may have. He may have heard me mention it, or father may have told him. Paul always drank chocolate when he played chess with father."

"That will serve." Another finger. "The second fact. Kalmus knew what the arrangements were. He knew that Jerin would be alone in the library, and that he would be a messenger and so would have an opportunity to use the arsenic. Did he?"

"I don't know, but he must have. Father must have told all of them, the messengers."

Another finger. "The third fact. Kalmus knew that investigation would disclose an acceptable motive for your father. He knew of your association with Jerin and of your father's attitude toward it. Did he?"

"He knew I knew Paul, of course. But my father's attitude—if you mean he might have wanted to kill him, that's just silly. He thought he was—well, what you called him yourself, a freak."

"He disapproved of your associating with him?"

"He disapproved of my associating with various people. But he certainly didn't have any—"

"If you please." Wolfe snapped it. "This isn't a court, and I'm not a prosecutor trying to convict your father. I'm merely asking if Kalmus knew that inquiry would reveal circumstances that could be regarded as a possible motive for your father. I take it that he did. Yes?"

"Well . . . yes."

"That will do. So much for the facts. I call them facts because if one or more of them can be successfully challenged my theory is untenable. Now the surmises, two of them. They can't be tested, merely stated. They are desirable but not essential. First, Kalmus knew that your father would himself take the chocolate to Jerin. Ideally, he suggested it, but I'll take less than the ideal. Second, when Mr. Yerkes brought word that Jerin was indisposed, Kalmus suggested to your father that it might be well to dispose of the pot and cup. Since Kalmus was a messenger, he had had opportunity to observe that Jerin had drunk most of the chocolate. And he ran no risk of arousing suspicion of his good faith. Since Jerin had been taken ill suddenly, it was a natural precaution to suggest. You said yesterday that your father told you and your mother exactly what had happened. Did he say that anyone had suggested that he see to the pot and cup?"

"No." Sally's fists were so tight I could see the white on her knuckles. "I don't believe it, Mr. Wolfe. I *can't* believe it. Of course Archie was right, I thought Dan Kalmus might want . . . I thought he wouldn't do everything he could, everything he ought to do . . . but now you're saying he killed Paul, he *planned* it, so my father would be arrested and convicted. I *can't* believe it!"

"You need not. As I said, I specified Kalmus only to avoid verbal complexities. It could have been one of the others—Hausman, Yerkes, Farrow—or even the cook or steward, though they are less probable. He must fit my three facts, and he should be eligible for my two surmises. Above all, he must meet the most obvious requirement, that he had a compelling reason to wish to ruin your father, to take his liberty if not his life. Does any of the others qualify? Hausman, Yerkes, Farrow, the cook, or steward?"

She shook her head. Her mouth opened and shut, but no words came.

"One of them might, of course, without your knowledge. But that was another reason for specifying Kalmus; you had yourself supplied a possible inducement for him. And now, with this theory, I must of course see him in any case. If he is guiltless and is proceeding on the assumption that the death of Jerin was the sole and final objective of the murderer, unless I intervene your father is doomed. It may be that the fact known only to Kalmus and your father, mentioned in the note to your mother which Mr. Goodwin read, is relevant, but speculation on that would be futile. I must see Mr. Kalmus, peccant or not, and for that I need your help." He swiveled. "Your notebook, Archie."

I got it, and my pen. "Shoot."

"Just a draft for Miss Blount. Any paper, no carbon. She will supply the salutation. I suppose my mother has told you that I am at Nero Wolfe's house, comma, and I am going to stay here until I am sure I have done all I can for my father. Period. Mr. Wolfe has a theory you should know about, comma, and you must come and talk with him tomorrow, comma, Wednesday. Period. He will be here all day and evening, comma, but is not available from nine to eleven in the morning and from four to six in the afternoon. Period. If you haven't come by noon Thursday I shall see a newspaper reporter and tell him why I came here and why I don't trust you to represent my father effectively."

He turned to her. "From you to Mr. Kalmus, handwritten. On my letterhead or plain paper, as you prefer. Mr. Goodwin will take it to his office after lunch."

"I won't," she said positively. "I couldn't tell a reporter that. I *couldn't*. I won't."

"Certainly you won't. You won't have to. He'll come."

"But if he doesn't?"

"He will. If he doesn't we'll try something else. Notify him that you have engaged an attorney to take legal steps to have him superseded as your father's counsel. I'm not a lawyer, but I know a good one, and the law has room for many stratagems." He flattened his palm on the desk. "Miss Blount. I shall see Mr. Kalmus, or quit. As you please."

"Not quit." She looked at me. "How does it . . . will you read it, Archie?"

I did so, including commas and periods.

She shook her head. "It's not like me. He'll know I didn't write it." She looked at Wolfe. "He'll know you did."

"Certainly he will. That is intended."

"Well." She took a breath. "But I won't tell any reporter, no matter what happens."

"That is *not* intended." Wolfe twisted his head to look up at the wall clock. "Before you write it, please make a phone call or two. Mr. Yerkes, Mr. Farrow, Dr. Avery. It's just as well I didn't see them before Mr. Cramer brought me that fact; it would have been wasted time and effort. Can you get them to come? At six o'clock or, preferably, after dinner, say at nine-thirty. Either separately or together."

"I can try. What phone do I use? There isn't one in my room."

Wolfe's lips tightened. A woman saying casually "my room," meaning a room in his house, was hard to take. I told her she could use my phone and went to get another chair to sit on while I typed the letter to Kalmus for her to copy.

7

Usually I know exactly what Wolfe is doing while he's doing it, and why. I always know afterwards exactly what he did, and nearly always I know why. But I'm still not dead sure, months later, that I know why he had Sally phone those guys and get them to come that day. At the time I not only wasn't sure, I couldn't even guess. He hates to work. When I return from an errand on a case and sit down to report, and he knows he must listen and listen hard, from the look he gives me you might think I had put ketchup in his beer. When a caller enters the office, even if he expects to pry out of him some essential fact on a tough one, from the welcome he gets you might think he had come to examine the income tax reports for the past ten years.

So why ask Sally to get people to work on both before and after dinner, before he had had a go at the most likely candidate? I didn't get it. I now believe that though he wasn't aware of it, he was grabbing at straws. He was pretending, not only to Sally and me but also to himself, that the new situation, resulting from the fact Cramer had brought, was just dandy because it gave him a new approach. But actually what it amounted to was that it was now extremely close to certain that none of the other candidates had had a shadow of a reason to kill Paul Jerin, and therefore it took either a mule or a sap to stick to the basic assumption that Blount hadn't. You can't sit and enjoy a book, even a fascinating one about what happened in

Africa a hundred thousand years ago, while you're fighting off a suspicion that you're acting like a mule or a sap, so you tell your client to get people to come to take your mind off your misery. As I say, I'm not dead sure, but I suspect that was it.

Of course it's barely possible that even at that stage he had some vague notion in some corner of his skull of what had really happened that night at the Gambit Club, but I don't think so. In that case he would have—but I'd better save that.

However, there wasn't much work to the first interview, before dinner, with Morton Farrow. Yerkes, the banker, had told Sally he would come around nine-thirty, but the best she could get out of Avery, the doctor, was that he would try to make it some time during the evening. It had been decided after lunch, after I returned from taking the letter to Kalmus' office—in a steel-and-glass fifty-story hive in the financial district where his firm had a whole floor—that Sally would not appear, and before six o'clock came she went up to her room. Farrow had said he would arrive at six but was twenty minutes late. I left it to Fritz to admit him, thinking he would consider it improper for a famous detective to answer a doorbell.

When Fritz ushered him to the office he came across to me with his hand out. I took it and let it go, and he turned to Wolfe, but Wolfe, who is always prepared for it, had turned to the Webster's New International Dictionary, Second Edition, leather-bound, on the stand at his elbow, and was busy turning pages. Farrow stood and watched him for five seconds and then turned back to me and boomed, "Where's Sally?" I told him she was upstairs and might be down later, and indicated the red leather chair, and, when he was seated and it was safe, Wolfe closed the dictionary and swiveled.

"Good evening," he said. "I'm Nero Wolfe. You told Miss Blount you couldn't stay long."

Farrow nodded. "I've got a dinner date." Twice as loud as necessary. He glanced at his wrist. "I'll have to trot along in half an hour, but that should be enough. I couldn't make it by six, couldn't get away. With the big boss gone I've got my hands full. I was glad Sally called me. She said you wanted to see me, and I wanted to see you. I know her, and of course you don't. She's a good kid, and I'm all for her, but like everybody else she has kinks. Apparently she has sold you a bill of goods. I'm a salesman myself, a sales manager for a hundred-million-dollar corporation, but it depends on what you're selling. Sally just doesn't understand her mother, my aunt, and never will. Of course that's strictly a family matter, but she's brought it into this mess herself, she's sold you on it, and I've got to set you straight. She's got you believing that there's something between my aunt and Dan Kalmus. That's plain moonshine. Anybody who knows my Auntyanna—have you ever seen her?"

"No." Wolfe was regarding him without enthusiasm.

"If she wanted to she could have something not only with Kalmus but with about any man she wanted to pick. I'm her nephew, so you might think I'm prejudiced, but ask anyone. But it's wasted on her because she's strictly a one-man woman, and she's married to the man. Sally knows that, she can't help but know it, but you know how it is with daughters. Or do you?"

"No."

"It's always one way or the other, either the mother is jealous of the daughter or the daughter is jealous of the mother. It never fails. Give me ten minutes with any mother and daughter and I'll tell you how it stands, and with my Auntyanna and Sally I've had years. This idea of Sally's, the idea that Kalmus will cross up Uncle Matt so he can make a play for her mother, that's pure crap. She may even think her mother knows it or suspects it but pretends not to. Does she?"

"No."

"I'll bet she does. A daughter jealous of a mother can think anything. So to protect her father she comes and hires you, and what good does that do? The fact remains that he arranged it, Jerin being there at the club, and he took the chocolate to him, and he got the cup and pot and washed them out. You may be a great detective, but you can't change the facts."

Wolfe grunted. "Then you think Mr. Blount is guilty."

"Of course I don't. I'm his nephew. I only say you can't change the evidence."

"I can try to interpret it. Are you a chess player, Mr. Farrow?"

"I play *at* it. I'm all right the first three or four moves, any opening from the Ruy Lopez to the Caro-Kann, but

I soon get lost. My uncle got me started at it because he thinks it develops the brain. I'm not so sure. Look at Bobby Fischer, the American champion. Has he *got* a brain? If I've developed enough to handle a hundred-million-dollar corporation, and that's what I've been doing for two weeks now, I don't think playing chess has helped me any. I'm cut out to be a top executive, not to sit and concentrate for half an hour and then push a pawn."

"I understand you didn't play one of the boards that evening, against Mr. Jerin."

"Hell no. He would have mated me in ten moves. I was one of the messengers. I was there in the library with Jerin, reporting a move from Table Ten, when Uncle Matt came up with the chocolate for him."

"On a tray. The pot, a cup and saucer, and a napkin."

"Yes."

"Did your uncle linger or did he leave at once, to return to the other room and his chessboard?"

"He didn't linger. He put the tray on the table and left. I've been over this several times with the police."

"Then you may oblige me in my attempt to interpret the evidence. It seems unlikely that Mr. Blount put arsenic in the chocolate while in the kitchen, since the steward and cook were there. He might have done it while mounting the stairs, which are steep and narrow, but it would have been awkward. He didn't do it after entering the library, for you were there and would have seen him, and after that he remained at his chessboard until word came that Jerin was ill. So his one opportunity was on the stairs, whereas each of the messengers had an opportunity each time he entered the library to report a move. Correct?"

"Not if I understand you." Farrow reversed his crossed legs. "Do you mean one of the messengers could have put the arsenic in the chocolate?"

"I do."

"With Jerin sitting right there? Right under his nose?"

"He might have closed his eyes to concentrate. I often do. Or he might have got up to pace the floor and turned his back."

"He might have, but he didn't. I went in there to report a move about thirty times, and he never moved from the couch, and his eyes were open. Anyway—of course you know who the messengers were, besides me?"

Wolfe nodded. "Mr. Yerkes, Mr. Kalmus, Mr. Hausman."

"Then how silly can you get? One of *them* poisoned the chocolate?"

"I'm examining the evidence. They had opportunity. You don't think it conceivable?"

"I certainly don't!"

"Indeed." Wolfe scratched his chin. "That leaves only the steward, Mr. Nash, and the cook, Mr. Laghi. Which one do you consider most likely?"

"Neither one." Farrow flipped a hand. "You realize I've been over all this, with the police and at the District Attorney's office. If there's any possible reason why Nash or Tony would have done it *I* don't know what it is, and the police would have dug it up."

"Then you exclude them?"

"If the cops do, I do."

"Then you're up a stump, Mr. Farrow. You've excluded everybody. No one put arsenic in the chocolate. Can you explain how it got into Mr. Jerin?"

"I don't have to. That's not up to me, it's up to the police." He uncrossed his legs. He looked at his watch. "All right, I came here to say something and I've said it. Before I leave I want to see my cousin. Where is she?"

Wolfe looked at me, putting it up to the supposed expert on women. It seemed to me that the situation called more for an expert on top executives, but I was for anything that might possibly give a gleam of light or hope, so I said I would ask her and got up and headed for the hall and the stairs. Mounting the two flights, I found that I wouldn't have to knock; she was there at the landing with her shoes on. Halting on the third step from the top, I asked her, "Could you hear?"

"I wasn't trying to," she said. "I was wanting to go down, but Mr. Wolfe said not to. Of course I could hear his voice. What does he say?"

"He's a psychologist. He says you have kinks. He says it's always one way or the other, either the mother is jealous of the daughter or the daughter is jealous of the mother, and a daughter jealous of a mother can think anything. He wants to see you before he goes, probably to straighten out a kink or two, and if you would like—"

"What does he say about Dan Kalmus?"

"That's one of your kinks. Your idea about Kalmus is pure crap. You may even—"

She moved. I had to either sidestep or get bumped, so I made room for her to get by, and had another look at the nice shoulders and the neck curve as I followed her down. As we entered the office Farrow twisted around in his chair and then arose, and apparently he intended to give her a cousinly kiss, but the look on her face stopped him. It certainly would have stopped me. He was starting, "Now look here, Sal, you—", but she stopped that also.

"You too," she said, with more scorch than I would have thought she had in her. "You would like it too, wouldn't you? You think she would have it all, she would own everything, and she would let you run it. You *would* think that, but you're wrong. You're always wrong. She would let *him* run it; that's what he's after, besides her. You're just a fool, a complete fool, you always have been."

She turned and went, to the door and on out. Farrow stood and gawked at her back, then wheeled to Wolfe, extended his hands, palms up, and waggled his head. "By God," he said, "there you are. Calling me a fool. What did I tell you? Calling *me* a fool!"

8

At the dinner table, and with coffee in the office afterwards, Wolfe resumed on the subject he had started at lunch— Voltaire. The big question was, could a man be called great on account of the way he used words, even though he was a toady, a trimmer, a forger, and an intellectual fop. That had been dealt with at lunch, and Voltaire had come out fairly well except on the toady count. How could you call a man great who sought the company and the favors of dukes and duchesses, of Richelieu, of Frederick of Prussia? But it was at dinner and in the office that Voltaire really got it.

What finally ruled him out was something that hadn't been mentioned at lunch at all: he had no palate and not much appetite. He was indifferent to food; he might even eat only once a day; and he drank next to nothing. All his life he was extremely skinny, and in his later years he was merely a skeleton. To call him a great man was absurd; strictly speaking, he wasn't a man at all, since he had no palate and a dried-up stomach. He was a remarkable word-assembly plant, but he wasn't a man, let alone a great one.

I suppose I shouldn't do this. I should either report Wolfe's table talk verbatim, and you could either enjoy it or skip it, or I shouldn't mention it. Usually I leave it out, but that evening I had a suspicion that I want to put in. Reporting to him on my visit to the Blount apartment, I had of course included a description of Kalmus: mostly bones and skin. I suspected that that was why Wolfe picked on Voltaire for both lunch and dinner, leading up to the climax. It wasn't much of a connection, but it was a connection, and it showed that he couldn't forget the fix he was in even at meals. That was my suspicion, and, if I was right, I didn't like it. It had never happened before. It had to mean that he was afraid that sooner or later he was going to have to eat something highly unpleasant for both his palate and his stomach—the assumption that Matthew Blount was innocent.

The coffee things were still there and he was still on Voltaire when Charles W. Yerkes came a little before nine-thirty. Another indication of Wolfe's state of mind was when the doorbell rang and Sally asked him if she should leave, and he raised his shoulders an eighth of an inch and said, "As you please." That wasn't him at all, and, as I went to the front to admit the caller, I had to arrange my face not to give him the impression that what we needed was sympathy and plenty of it.

Sally had stood when I went to answer the bell, and she met Yerkes at the office door. He took her offered hand in both of his, murmuring something, gave her hand a pat and let it go, and shot a glance to right and left as he entered. When Wolfe didn't extend a hand of course he didn't; he *was* a top executive. They exchanged nods as I pronounced names, and he waited until Sally was seated, in one of the yellow chairs I had moved up, to take the red leather one. As he sat he spoke, to her. "I came because I said I would, Sally, but I'm a little confused. After you phoned I called your mother, and apparently there's a . . . a misunderstanding. She seems to think you're making a mistake."

Sally nodded. "Did she tell you what I—why I'm here?"

"Only vaguely. Perhaps you'll tell me, so I'll know why *I'm* here." He was smiling at her, friendly but wanting to know. Cagey, but why not? A senior vice-president of a billion-dollar bank who is involved in a front-page murder case, even accidentally, isn't going to get involved any deeper if he can help it. Also he was good at chess.

"I *don't* think I'm making a mistake," Sally said. "The reason I'm here is . . . because I . . ." She let it hang, turned her head to look at me, and then looked at Wolfe. "Will you tell him, Mr. Wolfe?"

Wolfe was leaning back, his eyes at Yerkes. "I presume, sir, you're a man of discretion."

"I like to think I am." At Wolfe, the banker wasn't smiling. "I try to be."

"Good. The circumstances require it. It's merely a difference of opinion, but it would be unfortunate if it were made public at the moment. You may have seen an item in a newspaper yesterday that I have been engaged to inquire into the murder of Paul Jerin."

"It was called to my attention."

"It was Miss Blount who engaged me, against the advice of her father and his attorney, and her mother agrees with them. She offered me a sizable fee and I took it. Knowing that her father is in serious jeopardy, she fears that his counsel is not up to the emergency, and she has a high regard for my talents, possibly exaggerated. In making an inquiry I need to inquire, and you are one of those concerned in the matter. Mrs. Blount thinks her daughter has made a mistake in hiring me, but her daughter doesn't and I don't. My self-esteem rejects any supposition that I'll be a hindrance. I may conceivably hit upon a point that Mr. Kalmus would miss—not that I challenge his competence, though he decries mine. Have I made it clear—why Miss Blount asked you to come?"

"Not entirely. Of course I have been questioned by law officers, and by Mr. Kalmus, but I could contribute nothing useful." Yerkes's eyes went to Sally, shifting around ninety degrees while his head hardly moved at all. It's a good

trick for a shoplifter or pickpocket because it helps on secu-
rity, and it's probably also good at directors' meetings because it saves energy. He asked her, "Why do you think
Dan isn't up to it, Sally? Any particular reason?"

Either Mrs. Blount hadn't mentioned the problem of
jealous daughters or he was being discreet. Sally did all right.
"No," she said, "not particular. I'm just . . . *afraid.*"

"Well." His quick keen eyes went back to Wolfe. "Frankly,
Wolfe, I'm inclined to agree with them. My bank doesn't
happen to use Kalmus's firm, and neither do I personally, but
he certainly is a reputable lawyer, and as far as I know an
able one. What can you do that he can't do?"

"I won't know until I've done it." Wolfe straightened up.
"Mr. Yerkes. Do you think Mr. Blount killed that man?"

"Of course not. Certainly not." But before he said it his
eyes darted a glance at Sally, a dead giveaway. If he had
really felt and meant that "of course not" why glance at
her? Either he simply didn't mean it or he was an extremely smooth customer who knew more tricks than one and
also knew more about the death of Paul Jerin than he was
supposed to. He didn't add one of the old stand-bys, such
as that he had known Blount for many years and he
wouldn't kill a fly.

"Neither do I," Wolfe said, as if he did mean it. "But the
factual evidence pointing to him is weighty and can't be
impeached. You know that?"

"Yes."

"So I ignore it. There are other facts—for instance, that
four other men, the four messengers, had opportunities to
poison the chocolate, when they entered the library to report
moves. I understand that on those occasions, some if not all,
Jerin closed his eyes to concentrate. Is that true?"

"Yes. Usually he did, after the first three or four moves.
He bent his head down and sometimes covered his eyes
with his hands." Yerkes turned to the client. "You understand,
Sally, my answering these questions doesn't mean that I'm
siding with you against your father and mother. I'm not. But
you have a right to your opinion, and I'm willing to
oblige you within reason." Back to Wolfe. "And I agree
that you're not likely to be a hindrance. I know something
of your record. But Kalmus is quite aware that the four
messengers had plenty of opportunities, including me. That's

obvious. The question is, why would I? Why would any of them?"

Wolfe nodded. "That's the point. Take you. You had no animus for Mr. Jerin. But it's conceivable that you had, and still have, ill will toward Mr. Blount. And Jerin's death was only one of two dismal consequences of his drinking that chocolate; the other is that Blount is in deadly peril. Is that somehow pleasing to you, Mr. Yerkes? I have been hired to make an inquiry and I'm inquiring. Did you perhaps suggest to Blount that he should himself take the chocolate to Jerin? Or, when you informed him that Jerin was unwell, did you suggest that he should attend to the pot and cup?"

The banker's eyes were narrowed, and his lips were tight. "I see," he said, low, so low that I barely got it, and I have good ears. "That's how you . . . I see." He nodded. "Very clever. Possibly more than clever. Kalmus may have it in mind too—I don't know. You asked me two questions—no, three. The answer is no to all of them. But you have certainly hit on a point. This makes it . . . hmmm . . . Hausman, Farrow, and Kalmus . . . hmmm. Of course I have no comment." He turned to Sally. "But I'm not so sure you made a mistake." Back to Wolfe. "I do understand you? You're saying that Jerin was merely a pawn to be sacrificed in a deliberate plot to destroy Blount?"

"I'm suggesting it. It's my working hypothesis. Naturally you said no to my three questions; so would the other three. You would also say no if I asked you whether you have any knowledge of their relations with Blount that would be suggestive; and so would they. But a man's feeling toward another so intense that he is bent implacably on his ruin—such a feeling doesn't exist in a vacuum. It has discoverable roots, and I intend to find them. Or the feeling, intense feeling, might not be directed at Blount; it might be fastened on some desired object which only Blount's removal would render accessible. With Farrow, it might be control of an industrial empire, through his aunt; with Hausman, who is by nature fanatic, it might be some grotesque aspiration; with you or Kalmus, it might be Mrs. Blount. I intend—"

"Mrs. Blount's daughter is present, Wolfe."

"So she is. I'm only speculating at random. I didn't inject Mrs. Blount's name wantonly; Mr. Goodwin, who has seen her and who is qualified to judge, says that she might well unwittingly lead a man to defy the second prescription of the Tenth Commandment, thou shalt not covet thy neighbor's wife. But I am only speculating. I intend to find the roots. I haven't the legions of the law, but I have three good men available besides Mr. Goodwin, and there is no pressing urgency. Mr. Blount won't be brought to trial this week or month."

He was talking to hear himself, rambling on about vacuums and roots and quoting the Bible. He hadn't the faintest notion that Charles W. Yerkes had murdered Paul Jerin in order to erase Matthew Blount, nor did he expect to get any drop of useful information from that bimbo. Merely he would rather talk than try some other way of occupying his mind to keep it off of the fix he was in.

At that, he had a good listener. Yerkes wasn't missing a word. When Wolfe paused for breath he asked, "Have you suggested this working hypothesis to the District Attorney's office?"

Fine. A satisfactory answer to that, with a full explanation, would take a good three minutes. But Wolfe only said, "No, sir. They're satisfied with Mr. Blount. I am not."

Yerkes looked at Sally and then at me, but he wasn't seeing us; he was merely giving his eyes a change from Wolfe while he decided something. It took him some seconds, then he returned to Wolfe. "You realize," he said, "that for a senior officer of an important financial institution the publicity connected with an affair like this is . . . regrettable. Even a little . . . embarrassing. Of course it was proper and necessary for the police to see some of my friends and associates, to learn if I had had any kind of connection with that man Jerin, but it has been disagreeable. And now you, your men, private detectives, inquiring into my relations with Blount—that could be even more disagreeable, but I know I can't stop you. I admit your hypothesis is at least plausible. But I can save you some time and trouble, and perhaps make it less disagreeable for me."

He paused to swallow; it wasn't coming easy. "It is common knowledge in the banking world that before long a choice will be made for a new president of my bank, and that I will probably be named, but some of the directors, a minority, at present favor another man. Matthew Blount is one of that minority, but naturally since he is now . . . in the circumstances, he will not be able to attend the Board meeting next week. It wouldn't have taken much inquiry for you to learn this, hundreds of people know it, but I want to add that it has had no effect on my personal relations with Blount. It isn't that he's against me, it's only that he has greater obligations to the other man, and I understand it and so does he. I will *not* add that I didn't kill that man Jerin with the purpose of getting Blount charged with murder; I won't dignify anything so fantastic by denying it."

He rose. "I wish you luck with your hypothesis. The other three, Hausman and Farrow and Kalmus, are merely men I know, but Matthew Blount is my old and valued friend, and so is his wife." He moved, to Sally. "So are you, Sally. I think you should go home, that's where you belong at a time like this. I'm sure your father would want—"

The doorbell rang. I could have left it to Fritz, since he was still in the kitchen and it wasn't ten o'clock yet, but I had to go to the hall anyway to see Yerkes out, so I went. There had been no picture in the papers of Victor Avery, M.D., but if you're expecting an upper-bracket doctor to drop in and you see on the stoop a middle-aged well-fed specimen in a conventional gray overcoat, with scarf, and a dark gray homburg, when you open the door you greet him politely, "Dr. Avery?"

As he removed the coat, with an assist from me, Yerkes came, followed by Sally, and I observed that apparently Avery was just another man Yerkes knew, not an old and valued friend; or it may have been only that Yerkes's mind was too occupied for more than a word and a nod, and Avery's attention was all for Sally. He took her hand and patted her arm and said, "My *dear* child," and let the hand go only when they reached the office door. When I joined them in the office after closing the door behind Yerkes, Avery was in the red leather chair and speaking, telling Sally that he had turned a matter over to an assistant so he could come. I noticed as I passed, looking down at him, that he had just the right amount of gray in his hair to look the part.

He turned to Wolfe. "There aren't many things I wouldn't do for Miss Blount. In fact I feel responsible, since I brought her into the world. So I'm here, at your disposal, though I don't know exactly what for. She told me on the phone that she has employed you in her father's interest—professionally. If that's correct—to call a detective a professional man?"

Wolfe nodded. "The dictionary would permit it."

"Good enough. Miss Blount also told me that you're acting independently of her father's attorney. That seems to me a little difficult, a little awkward, but I'm not qualified to judge. The only profession I know anything about is medicine. She said you wanted to see me, and here I am. I would go much farther, to see the devil himself, if it might be of assistance to Miss Blount's father."

Wolfe grunted. "Do you think he killed Paul Jerin?"

"No. I do not." He didn't glance at Sally as Yerkes had. "How long have you been a member of the Gambit Club?"

"Fifteen years."

"How well do you know Mr. Hausman?"

"Not well at all. I rarely see him except at the club. I see him once every year on Matthew Blount's birthday. Mrs. Blount gives a party."

"How well do you know Mr. Yerkes?"

"Not much better than I know Hausman. Except at the club, only casually."

"Mr. Farrow?"

"I know *him*, certainly. You know he is Mrs. Blount's nephew."

"Yes. Mr. Kalmus?"

"I have known him for years. Aside from our friendship, I attend him professionally." Avery shifted in the chair, settling back. "Those four men were the messengers, as of course you know."

"Of course. More of them later. First the event itself. I understand it was Mr. Kalmus who summoned you to go to Mr. Jerin."

"That's right. But I knew before that that Jerin was indisposed, about half an hour before, when Yerkes told Blount. I was at Table Five, next to Blount, Table Six."

"It was then that Blount went to the library to take the pot and cup and clean them."

"That's right."

"Did Yerkes suggest to Blount that he do that?"

"I don't think so. If he did I didn't hear him."

"Did anyone else suggest it?"

"I don't think so, but I don't know. Yerkes was the messenger for our tables, and he had brought me Jerin's sixth move, and I was concentrating on my reply. I was trying the Albin Counter Gambit. Houghteling had used it against

Dodge in 1905 and had mated him on the sixteenth move. But perhaps you don't play chess."

"I don't know that gambit." From Wolfe's tone, he didn't care to. "When you went in to Jerin, having been summoned by Kalmus, did you suspect poison at once?"

"Oh no, not at once. There was faintness, depression, and some nausea, and those symptoms can come from a variety of causes. It was only when he complained of intense thirst, and his mouth was dry, that I considered the possibility of poison, specifically arsenic, but the clinical picture of arsenical poisoning is by no means always the same. As a precaution I sent to a nearby drugstore for mustard, tinctura ferri chloridi, and magnesium oxide, and when they came I administered mustard water, but not the tincture. That's the official arsenic antidote, and it should be used only after gastric lavage and a test of the washings. Of course there was no equipment at the club for that, and, when the symptoms became more acute, I sent for an ambulance and he was taken to a hospital. St. Vincent's."

"You continued in attendance at the hospital?"

Avery nodded. "With members of the staff. They took over, actually."

"But you were present?"

"Yes. Until he died."

"At what point did he know he had been poisoned?"

"That's hard to say." Avery pursed his lips. "When I went to him he thought there had been something wrong with the chocolate, naturally, since he had taken nothing else, and of course anything swallowed by a man that makes him ill is toxic, but it was only after he had been at the hospital for some time that he voiced a suspicion that he had been poisoned deliberately. You asked when he *knew*. He never did know, but he suspected it."

"Did he name anyone? Accuse anyone?"

"I prefer not to say."

"Pfui. Did he name someone only in your hearing?"

"No."

"Did he name someone in the hearing of yourself and another?"

"Yes. Others."

"Then the police know about it, and presumably Mr. Kalmus. Why shouldn't I know?"

Avery turned, slowly, to look at Sally. "I haven't told you,

Sally," he said, "nor your mother. But of course the police have been told—a doctor and two nurses were there and heard it. You asked me to come to see Wolfe, so I suppose you want him to know. Do you?"

"Yes," Sally said, "I want him to know everything."

Avery regarded her a moment, opened his mouth and closed it, turned to Wolfe, and said, "He named Blount."

"What did he say?"

"He said—these were his words: 'Where's that bastard Blount? He did this, he did it. Where is he? I want to see him. Where is the bastard?' Of course he was raving. It meant absolutely nothing. But he said it, and the police know it." Back to Sally: "Don't tell your mother. It wouldn't do any good, and it's hard enough for her without that."

Sally, staring at him, was shaking her head. "Why would he . . ." She looked at me, and I had to say something. "Nuts," I said. "He was off the rails." Having already swallowed a full-grown camel, though it was tough keeping it down, I wasn't going to strain at a gnat.

Wolfe, focused on Avery, asked, "Did he elaborate on that?"

"No. That was all."

"Or repeat it?"

"No."

"Was he questioned about it? By you or another?"

"No. He was not in a condition to be questioned."

"Then as information it has no value. To go back to the club. You said that when you went to him he thought there had been something wrong with the chocolate, and naturally you shared that suspicion. Did you make any inquiry?"

"Yes, but it was fruitless because none of the chocolate that he had taken was left. The pot and cup had been taken —but you know about that. I went down to the kitchen and questioned the cook and steward and looked around some. However, I didn't do the one thing I should have done, and I regret it; I regret it deeply. I should have asked Jerin if he had put anything in the chocolate that he had brought with him. At the time that possibility didn't occur to me, since he was saying there must have been something wrong with the chocolate as it was served. It only occurred to me later, two days later, when it developed that Blount was seriously suspected of deliberate murder. If I had been fully alert to the possibilities of the situation then and there, at the club,

I would have questioned Jerin insistently. I would even have searched him, his pockets. I regret it deeply."

"Are you suggesting that he committed suicide? And then, at the point of death, accused Blount?"

"Not necessarily suicide. That's conceivable, but more likely, he put something in the chocolate which he believed to be innocuous but wasn't. It could have been some stimulant, either powder or liquid, or it could even have been some special form of sugar he fancied. And either by mistake or through the malign purpose of some other person, arsenic in one of its many forms had been substituted for the harmless substance. Of course it would have had to be in some kind of container, and I went to the club to search and inquire, but two days had passed and the police had already made a thorough inspection. The library had been put in order by the steward Tuesday night and the wastebasket emptied. I have been told by the police that there was no container on Jerin's person, but they don't really know, since he was undressed soon after his arrival at the hospital."

Wolfe grunted. "So all you have is a conjecture that can't be supported."

"I'm not so sure, and I'm sorry you say that." Avery was leaning forward. "Your attitude is the same as Kalmus's when I made the suggestion to him. Kalmus is an able lawyer, a brilliant lawyer, but naturally his approach to any problem is the *legal* approach. You're right, my idea is no good if it can't be supported, but that's just the point, perhaps it *can* be supported, and that's why I wanted to tell you about it, because it's a job for a detective, not a lawyer. I won't try to tell *you* the dozen different ways it *might* be supported because that's your profession, not mine. But I'll say this, if I were a detective trying to get evidence that would clear Blount of the murder he has been charged with, which he didn't commit, or at least raise a strong enough doubt, I certainly wouldn't ignore this as a conjecture that can't be supported. I don't want to be importunate, but you realize I'm deeply concerned."

"Naturally." Wolfe was patient. "I concede that your suggestion is worth considering. It has the great merit that if it can be established it will clear not only Blount but also the others who had access to the chocolate—the four messengers. I said more of them later. A detective must consider them too. You have advanced a suggestion; now I offer one. One of those four men killed Jerin, not because of any malice toward him, but to destroy Blount. The malice was for Blount. That's why I asked how well you know them. If it can be shown—"

"Good lord." Avery was gawking. "That's tommyrot. You're not serious?"

"Why not? My suggestion is as worthy of consideration as yours and can be more easily investigated. Why is it tommyrot?"

"Why . . ." Avery turned his palms up. "Perhaps I should have said . . . implausible. To kill a man like that, deliberately, a man who means nothing to you, in an attempt to injure another man . . . I may be naïve for a man of my age and experience, but such depravity . . . it's hard for me to believe. I can't deny that it's conceivable."

"Then it's not tommyrot. But apparently it would be futile to ask if you have any knowledge or suspicion that would single out one of them."

"It certainly would." He was emphatic. "Even if I had any I wouldn't—" He stopped abruptly, looked at Sally, and returned to Wolfe. "No, that isn't true. If I had any such knowledge or suspicion I'd tell you. Have you any?"

Wolfe shook his head. "If I have I'm reserving it. I have spoken with three of them—Hausman, Farrow, and Yerkes —and I expect to see Kalmus tomorrow. They all profess belief in Blount's innocence, which is gratifying but not helpful. I not only profess it, I am committed to it; and whether through your suggestion or mine, or by some device not yet conceived, I intend to demonstrate it."

Hooray.

9

Daniel Kalmus, counselor at law, arrived a little after noon Wednesday. It was a good thing he didn't put it off until after lunch, as some extra fine lamb kidneys, skewered to keep them open, doused in olive oil seasoned with salt, pepper, thyme, dry mustard, and mace, broiled five-and-three —five minutes on the skin side and three minutes on the cut side—and brushed twice with deviled butter, would have been practically wasted. I have said that Wolfe refuses to let anything whatever spoil a meal if the food is good, but that day, if there had been no reaction whatever, not even a phone call, to Sally's ultimatum to Kalmus, the kidneys would of course have been chewed and swallowed, but they wouldn't have been appreciated. They might as well have been served to Voltaire.

That was the first and only time Wolfe has given me instructions and then canceled them, without anything having happened to change his mind. While Sally and I were having breakfast, fresh-baked croissants and eggs poached in red wine and bouillon, he buzzed me on the house phone from his room and told me to call Saul Panzer, Fred Durkin, and Orrie Cather—the three good men he had mentioned to Yerkes—and ask them to come at six o'clock. That improved my appetite for breakfast. I hadn't the dimmest notion what he was going to have them do, but it couldn't be just to ask their opinion of Dr. Avery's suggestion, since together they came to twenty-five bucks an hour. Then only ten minutes later he buzzed me again and told me to skip it. Absolutely unheard of. If there's one thing he never does it's toss and turn. A hell of a way to start a day.

When he came down to the office at eleven o'clock and saw the client there, in a chair over by the filing cabinet, with the *Times*, he paused on the way to his desk to scowl at her for a couple of seconds, acknowledged her good morn-

ing with a curt nod, switched the scowl to me, went and
put orchids in the vase, sat, removed the paperweight, a
chunk of petrified wood, from the little pile of morning mail,
and picked up the first item, a letter from the president of a
women's club in Montclair asking if and when about a hundred of the members could come and look at the orchids. I
had considered withholding it and answering it myself, in
view of his current acute feeling about club members, but
had decided that if I could take it he could.

He looked through the mail, put the paperweight back on
it, and looked at me. "Any phone calls?"

He never asked that, knowing as he did that if there had
been a call which he would want or need to know about I
would report it without being asked. So I said, "Yes, sir.
Lon Cohen wants to send a man to interview Miss Blount."

"Why did you tell him she's here?"

"I didn't. You know damn well I didn't. She went for a
walk and some journalist probably saw her and tailed her.
We can get Saul and Fred and Orrie and have them find out."

"Archie. I am in no mood for raillery."

"Neither am I."

His eyes went to his client. "Miss Blount. When Mr.
Kalmus comes you will of course retire before he enters."

"I'd rather stay," she said. "I want to."

"No. Mr. Goodwin will tell you later what was said. You
will please withdraw."

She shook her head. "I'm going to stay." Not arguing, just
stating a fact.

If he had been anything like normal he would have ex-
ploded, and if she had stuck to it he would have instructed
me to carry her upstairs and lock her in. Instead, he merely
glared at her, and then at me, removed the paperweight
from the mail, picked up the top letter, and growled, "Your
notebook, Archie."

In the next hour he dictated sixteen letters, only three of
them in reply to items that had come that morning. I still
have the notebook, and it's quite an assortment. Though
they all got typed, nine of them were never signed and
mailed. They were all quite polite. One, to a boy in Wichita,
Kansas, apologized for not answering his letter, received two
weeks back, asking two pages of questions about detective
work, but he didn't go so far as to answer the questions. He
was in the middle of one to an orchid hunter in Ecuador

when the doorbell rang; I stepped to the hall for a look, and turned to inform him, "Kalmus." It was ten minutes past noon.

Naturally I was curious to see how Sally would handle it, so when I ushered the caller to the office and he entered I was right behind. She stayed put, on the chair over by the cabinet, looking straight at him, but obviously not intending to move or speak. He was going to her but stopped halfway, muttered at her, "You silly little goose," and about-faced. His eyes met Wolfe's at eight paces, and I pronounced names and indicated the red leather chair. Kalmus spoke. "So you got me here with a threat from a hysterical girl."

That wasn't so easy to meet, since Wolfe thinks that any calm and quiet woman is merely taking time out from her chronic hysteria, building up for the next outbreak. So he ignored it. "Since you *are* here," he said, with no heat, "you might as well be seated. Eyes at a level are equal. Of course that's why a judge's bench is elevated."

Kalmus went to the red leather chair, but he didn't settle in it; he just perched on the front half of the seat. "I want to make one thing clear," he declared. "If you think you can force me to take you as a colleague in handling the defense of Matthew Blount, you're wrong. Anything I do or don't do, I'll decide it strictly on the only proper ground, is it in the interest of my client or isn't it. Also I want to say that I'm not surprised at the tactics you're using. It was partly because I know how you operate that I was against hiring you. I don't blame Miss Blount because she doesn't know any better. She doesn't know that coercion by threat partakes of the nature of blackmail, or that if she did what she threatened to do it would be libel. You can't deny that she wrote that letter at your direction."

Wolfe nodded. "I dictated it to Mr. Goodwin, he typed it, and she copied it." From his expression as he regarded the lawyer you might have thought he was merely trying to decide whether I had exaggerated about skin and bones. "As for blackmail, the only thing extorted is half an hour or so of your time. As for intent to libel, her defense would be the truth of the libel, but I concede that she couldn't possibly prove it. For you and me to discuss it would be pointless. She mistrusts your good faith as her father's counsel because she thinks you are capable of betraying him for your personal advantage, and of course you deny it. The question is moot and can't be resolved, so why waste time and words on it? What I would—"

"It's ridiculous! Childish nonsense!"

"That may be. You're the only one who knows the real answer, since it is inside you, your head and heart. What I would like to discuss is the theory Miss Blount mentioned in her letter. It is based partly on a conclusion from established fact and partly on an assumption. The assumption is that Mr. Blount is innocent. The conclusion is that—"

"I know all about the theory."

Wolfe's brows went up. "Indeed?"

"Yes. If it's what you told Yerkes last evening. Is it?"

"It is."

"He told me about it this morning. Not on the phone—he came to my office. He was impressed by it, and so am I. I was impressed when it first entered my mind, a week ago, and when I told Blount about it he too was impressed. I didn't do what you have done—speak of it to those who may be vitally concerned—at least one of them may be. Have you also told Farrow and Hausman?"

Wolfe's brows were still up. "It had already occurred to you?"

"Certainly. It had to. If Blount didn't put arsenic in that chocolate, and he didn't, it had to be one of those three, and he had to have a reason. I don't have to tell you that when a crime is committed the first and last question is *cui bono?* And the only result of the murder of Jerin that could possibly have benefited one of those three was the arrest of Blount on a capital charge. Of course you include me on the list, and I don't. Is that why you told Yerkes? Because you think this idiotic idea of Miss Blount's points to me and he's out of it?"

"No. At present you seem the most likely, but none of them is out of it. I told Yerkes to get talk started. Not just talk about you and Mrs. Blount; even if Miss Blount's suspicion is valid you have probably been too discreet to give occasion for talk; talk about the other three and their relations with Blount. The success of any investigation depends mainly on talk, as of course you know." Wolfe turned a hand. "You may not need it. You have known all of them for years. You may already have an inkling, more than an inkling, and, combining it with the fact known only to you and Blount, you may have your case secure. If so you don't need me."

Kalmus put his hands on the chair arms to lever himself back on the seat, cocked his head, and closed his eyes to look at something inside. Facing the window beyond Wolfe's desk, he didn't look quite as bony as he had in the firelight in the Blount living room, but he looked older; he did have creases, slanting down from the corners of his mouth and nose.

His eyes opened. "I haven't got my case secure," he said.

"Hmmmm," Wolfe said.

"Not secure. That theory, it's obvious enough if Blount is innocent, but why are you so sure he is? I know why I am, but why are you?"

Wolfe shook his head. "You can't expect a candid answer to that, since we're not colleagues. But if I have no other ground there is this: if Blount is guilty I can't possibly earn the fee I have accepted from his daughter, and an unearned fee is like raw fish—it fills the stomach but is hard to digest. Therefore my client's father didn't kill that man."

"You happen to be right. He didn't."

"Good. It's gratifying to have concurrence from one who knows. It would be even more gratifying to be told *how* you know, but I can't expect you to tell me. Presumably it's the fact known only to you and Mr. Blount."

"That's partly it. Chiefly." Kalmus took a deep breath. "I'm going to ask you something. I'm going to see my client this afternoon. If I suggest to him that we engage you to investigate something, and he approves, will you do it? Investigate one particular matter under my direction?"

"I can't say. I doubt it. I would have to know first precisely what is to be investigated, and how much I would be restricted by the direction. You disapprove of my tactics on principle."

"But they get results. If you were satisfied on those two points would you accept?"

"If there were no conflict of interest, if Miss Blount approved, and if it were stated in writing that Mr. Blount is my client, not you, yes. What would I investigate?"

"That will have to wait until I consult Blount. Will you be available this evening?"

"Yes. But I'll commit myself, if at all, only upon written

request from Mr. Blount. I owe some deference to Miss Blount's opinion of your probity, right or wrong. She *is* my client. And what of your abrupt somersault regarding me?"

"It wasn't abrupt." Kalmus twisted in the chair to face Sally, started to say something, vetoed it, and returned to Wolfe. "The fact you've mentioned twice, the fact known only to Blount and me, required investigation—not the fact itself, but what it suggested. I thought I could handle it myself with the help of a couple of men in my office, but day before yesterday, Monday afternoon, I realized that it would take an expert investigator, and I decided to call on you. Then came that item in the paper, that you had been hired on behalf of Blount, and I thought you were trying to horn in, and my reaction to that was natural. But that evening Mrs. Blount phoned me that her daughter had hired you, so you weren't just trying to horn in, and when I went up there I intended to smooth it out and hire you myself, but you know what I ran into. That ridiculous idea of Miss Blount's. I admit I acted like a damn fool. It wasn't Goodwin's fault, or yours; it was hers."

He waved it away. "All right, that was stupid. Then yesterday that letter came, obviously drafted by you. I forced myself to look at it objectively, and I had to admit that from your viewpoint you were acting in the legitimate interest of the person who had hired you. And this morning when Yerkes came and told me what you said to him last evening, the theory that I already had myself, it was obvious that you weren't just making gestures to get a fee, you genuinely thought Blount was innocent. So I came here with the definite intention of engaging your services. It may not have sounded like it, the way I started off, but I still resented that letter and you can't blame me. I didn't do any abrupt somersault about you."

He got up and crossed over to Sally. "Where you got that fool notion," he said, "God only knows. If you have any sense at all you'll go home where you belong. Two different newspapers have phoned my office this morning to ask what you're doing at Nero Wolfe's house. For God's sake get some sense." He put out a hand, pulled it back, and wheeled to face Wolfe. "I'll see Blount this afternoon and you'll hear from me either this evening or tomorrow morning. He'll feel better if I tell him that you're sending his daughter home. Can I tell him that?"

"No, sir. I don't prescribe my clients' movements."

"Very well." He thought he was going to add something, decided he wasn't, and headed for the door. I followed him out, for the courtesies of the hall.

Back at the office door, I didn't enter because Sally was there on the sill. "Do you believe him?" she demanded. From her tone and expression it seemed likely that if I said yes I might get my face scratched, so I took her arm and turned her to escort her to the red leather chair, and darned if she didn't balk. She wasn't going to sit where it was still warm from Dan Kalmus. She jerked her arm away, stood at the corner of Wolfe's desk, and demanded, "Do *you* believe him?"

"Confound it," Wolfe snapped, "sit down! My neck isn't rubber."

"But if you're going—"

"Sit down!"

She turned, saw I had moved up a chair, sat, and said, "You said I would have to approve. Well, I don't. Not under his direction."

Wolfe regarded her, not with enthusiasm. "He made one excellent suggestion," he declared. "That I send you home. But if I put you out you probably wouldn't go home, there's no telling where you'd go, and I need you. I need you now, and I may need you again at any moment. I neither believe him nor disbelieve him." He turned. "Archie?"

I was back at my desk. "Pass," I told him. "If he's a liar he's good. If he's straight Sally's a goof, and I told her Monday evening that I'm with her all the way, so I'm prejudiced. I pass."

He grunted. To her, "You heard me. I told him I would have to be satisfied about the direction. What do you want, Miss Blount? Did you hire me to discredit Mr. Kalmus or to clear your father?"

"Why . . . my father, of course."

"Then don't interfere. If there really is an important fact known only to Kalmus and your father I may soon learn what it is, before I commit myself to Kalmus, and then I'll decide what to do. He has by no means convinced me of his integrity, and I'm going to spend some of your money in an effort to verify or impeach your opinion of him. He is a widower?"

"Yes. His wife died ten years ago."

"He has children?"

She nodded. "Four. Two sons and two daughters. They're all married."

"Do any of them live with him? Or he with them?"

"No. He has an apartment on Thirty-eighth Street in a remodeled house that he owns. When the children got married and left he had it turned into apartments, one to a floor."

"Does he live alone?"

"Yes. He doesn't—"

"Yes is enough. Does he have servants? A servant?"

"Not to sleep in. A daily cleaning woman is all. He only eats breakfast—"

"If you please. Have you a key to his apartment?"

Her eyes widened. "Of course not. Why would I have a key?"

"I couldn't say. I merely ask." He turned. "Archie. Get Saul and Fred and Orrie. After lunch. Two-thirty if possible."

I swiveled and got the phone and dialed. Getting them in the middle of the day was doubtful, but Saul had an answering service, Fred had a wife, and for Orrie I had three different numbers, two of which were strictly his affair; and for Wolfe any and all of them would leave a job he happened to be on unless it was really hot.

I was at the phone off and on until lunchtime, and my meal was interrupted twice by call-backs from Fred and Orrie, but I wouldn't have minded if I had got no meal at all if necessary in order to get a ball rolling, though it did seem that Wolfe was piling it on. If all he had in mind was a tour of Kalmus's apartment, as was indicated by the questions he had asked Sally, why the platoon? Why not just send me? I had a suspicion and I didn't care for it. He wanted me around on account of Sally. With me not there to keep an eye on her, she might try to tell Fritz how to cook, or put tacks in Wolfe's bed, or change the furniture around. If that was it, if having her as a house guest meant that I would be sent on no errand if and when there was one, I was inclined to agree with Yerkes and Kalmus, at a time like this the place for her was home.

Bones were dwelt upon again at lunch, but not Voltaire's; these had been found in some gorge somewhere in Africa, and they proved that the chief difference between me and the galoots who put them there a million years ago was that I can use a typewriter; I *think* that was it. The kidneys were fully appreciated, and, as I was chewing my last one, Fritz stepped in after answering the doorbell to say that Mr. Panzer was there. If Sally hadn't been present he would of course have said Saul. By the time we finished with the salad and coffee Fred and Orrie had also come.

I had told them on the phone that Sally Blount would be present, and, when we entered the office and I introduced them to her, it was interesting, as it always is, to see how true they ran to form. Saul Panzer, five-feet-seven, 140 pounds, with a big nose and flat ears, not a good design for beauty, apparently looked casually in her direction only to be polite, but you could safely give a thousand to one that he had every little detail of her on file for good. Fred Durkin, five-feet-ten, 190 pounds, bald and burly, looked at her, then away, then back at her. He doesn't know he does that. Ever since the time, years ago, when he fell temporarily for a pretty little trick with ample apples, and his wife caught on, he doesn't trust himself with females under thirty. Orrie Cather, six-feet-flat, 180 pounds, good design from tip to toe, gave her a straight, honest, inquisitive, and acquisitive eye. He was born with the attitude toward all attractive women that a fisherman has toward all the trout in a stream, and has never seen any reason to change it.

Their three chairs lined up before Wolfe's desk didn't leave much space, and the red leather chair had had time to cool off from Kalmus, so Sally took it. Wolfe, after performing as usual with that trio, shaking hands with all of them because he wanted to with Saul, sat, moved his eyes left to right and back again, and spoke. "If it was troublesome for you to arrange to come I should thank you, and I do. I suppose you know what I'm concerned with—Matthew Blount, charged with the murder of Paul Jerin. You have just met his daughter. I won't describe the situation because for the present I have a single specific assignment for you. You probably know the name of Blount's lawyer: Daniel Kalmus."

Nods.

"There is reason to suspect that at some time prior to Tuesday evening, January thirtieth, he procured some arsenic somewhere; I have no slightest hint of where or how or when, but it was probably not more than a week or two before January thirtieth; it may well have been only a day or two. Note that I said 'reason to suspect'; that's all it is. Usually when I ask you to find something I have concluded that it exists; this time it's not a conclusion, merely a surmise. But you will spare no pains, and if you find it your fees will be doubled. Saul will be in charge and will direct you, but report here to Archie as usual."

He focused on Saul. "On such an operation you know how to proceed better than I do. I offer no suggestions. Evidence that he actually procured or possessed arsenic in some form would be most satisfactory, but even to establish that he had access to it would help substantially. Make no undue sacrifice to discretion; if he learns of your inquiries no harm will be done, for of course he has already taken all possible precautions. But you will exclude his doctor and his apartment. His doctor, Victor Avery, is his old and intimate friend; I have talked with him; and any approach to him or his office should be discussed with me beforehand. As for his apartment, it will be visited and inspected this evening by Archie, accompanied by Miss Blount. Miss Blount is an excellent source of information regarding his habits, haunts, associates—all about him. Get all you can from her first." He turned to her. "There are comfortable seats in the front room. If you please?"

She had fists again, her knuckles white. "But I told you . . . I just don't believe it . . ."

"You're not required to. I neither believe it nor reject it; I'm investigating. That's what you hired me for."

"You said I would go to his apartment with Archie. I *couldn't.*"

"We'll consider that later. In talking with Mr. Panzer, Mr. Durkin, and Mr. Cather, you need not disclose any matter which you wish to reserve. Mr. Goodwin will be with you." He turned. "Have your notebook, Archie."

I got it, arose, and headed for the door to the front room, and the trio got up and came, but stood aside at the door to let Sally go first. Ops appreciate a chance to be polite, they get so few. As I pulled the door shut a glance at Wolfe showed him reaching for *African Genesis*. Now that he was hard at work he could read again.

10

At ten minutes past ten that evening Sally and I got out of a taxi at the corner of Park Avenue and Thirty-eighth Street, walked a block and a half east with a gusty winter wind at our backs shoving us along, stood at the curb, and looked across the street at the windows of the fourth floor, the top, of a brick house painted gray with green trim. Seeing no sign of light, we crossed over, entered the vestibule, and inspected the row of names and buttons on the panel, and I pushed the button marked Kalmus, expecting no response, since I had dialed his phone number only a quarter of an hour ago and got no answer. After a thirty-second wait I pushed the button at the bottom, marked SUPERINTENDENT, and as I did so Sally gripped my arm.

It had taken some persuading to get her to come—in fact, more than persuading, since she had held out until Wolfe explained that if I came alone I would have to bring an assortment of keys and tools, and even if one of the keys worked I could be nailed for breaking and entering. Naturally that did it, since she was faced with the prospect of me in the coop and her there at Wolfe's mercy. The arrangement was that if and when Kalmus came to see Wolfe that evening Sally and I would not be visible, and after Fritz had escorted him to the office and shut the door we would take off on our errand, and Wolfe would keep him until word came from me that we were through. Also, if he hadn't shown by ten o'clock and his phone didn't answer, we would go anyhow and risk getting interrupted. On that I had fudged a little and dialed his number at nine-fifty.

So there we were in the vestibule. There was no receiver on a hook, just a pair of little circular grills in the wall at chin level, and after a brief wait there was a crackle and then a voice: "Who is it?" Sally, still gripping my arm,

spoke to the grill. "It's Sarah Blount. We want to see Mr.
Kalmus. We rang his bell, but he didn't answer. Do you
know where he is?"

"No, I don't."

"Well . . . we want to see him, but it's cold here in the
vestibule. May we wait inside? Will you let us in?"

"I guess so. I'll be up in a minute."

I put my hand to the door and kept it there, but there was
no click. A minute passed, and another, and still no click,
and then the door opened. The man who opened it, a thin
tall guy with a face as black as Jim Crow, made room for
us to enter, and when we were in let it shut. I knew more
about him, from Sally, than he did about me. His name was
Dobbs, and he had been the butler when the Kalmus family
had occupied the whole house.

He was frowning at Sally. "It's you all right, Miss Sarah,"
he said. "It's been so long since I saw you."

She nodded. "It certainly has. This is Mr. Goodwin. Mr.
Dobbs, Archie."

I offered a hand, and he took it. Of course shaking hands
with a butler is vulgar, but he wasn't a butler any more,
he was a superintendent.

"You haven't changed any," Sally said. "Except your hair.
All that gray." She was hating it, and I admit I couldn't
blame her.

"You have," Dobbs said, "but that's natural. You're on the
up, and I'm on the down. Will you permit me to say, I'm
sorry about your father's trouble. I know it's going to come
out all right, sure it will, but it's a big trouble." He looked at
me, and he had a good keen eye. "I know your name, you're
a detective." Back to Sally. "I guess that's why you want to
see Mr. Kalmus, your father's trouble."

"Yes, it is." For a moment I thought Sally was going to
flunk it, but she got it out: "Could we wait for him in his
apartment? Could you . . . would you . . . let us in? If we
have to wait long . . . we have to see him tonight . . ."

"Of course." After all, she had sat on his knee, with a
Kalmus daughter on the other knee, while he told them
stories, before the gray came to his hair—a detail I had got
from Sally. He said, "Mr. Kalmus wouldn't want *you* waiting
for him down here, that's sure," and headed for the open door
of the do-it-yourself elevator. Entering after us, he
pushed a button, the door closed, and we were lifted.

On the fourth floor the foyer was just a cell, four feet square, merely to provide walls for a door. Dobbs had taken a ring of keys from a pocket, but before he used one he pushed the button on the jamb and waited a full half a minute—in case Kalmus was in but had preferred not to answer our ring from downstairs. Evidently not. He used the key, opened the door, entered and flipped a wall switch, and there was light—plenty of it, though indirect, from troughs at the ceiling along two of the walls.

"There you are, Miss Sarah," he said. "It's not the way it used to be, is it?"

"No, it isn't, Dobbsy." She started a hand out but took it back. You don't shake the hand of a man you're tricking. But apparently it's all right to kiss him. Anyway, she did— a peck on the cheek—and said, "Did you hear that? Dobbsy!"

"You bet I heard it. You just bet I did." He bowed to her, and it could have been a butler bowing or an ambassador from somewhere in Africa. "I hope you don't have long to wait," he said, and went. When the door had closed behind him Sally flopped onto the nearest chair.

"My God," she groaned. "How awful. I didn't *want* to come. Will you hurry, Archie? Will you please hurry?"

I told her to relax, took my hat and coat off and dropped them on a chair, and glanced around. It was a big room, and by no means bare, and of course there would be a bedroom and bath, and a kitchenette. Even if I had been after some specific object like a bottle of arsenous oxide it would have been a three-hour job if done right, and since I expected nothing so obvious but merely hoped for something, no matter what, that would open a crack to let in a little light, the whole night wouldn't be too much. Say it was a single piece of paper, a letter or a record of something; one item alone, the books in the shelves that lined the wall on the right, to the ceiling, would take hours. And Kalmus might show any second. I decided to have a look at the bedroom first and started for a door at the left, but on the way I caught something from the corner of my eye and stopped and turned. Then I moved.

It was Kalmus. He was on the floor in front of a couch, and the couch hid him from view until you passed the end of it. He was fully dressed, on his back with his legs straight out. After glancing at Sally and seeing that she was still on the chair, her head bent forward and her face covered by her hands, I squatted. His eyes were open, staring at the ceiling, the pupils dilated, his face was purple, his tongue was sticking out, and there was dried froth around his mouth and nose. With the froth dry there was no use trying for a pulse or a breath. I poked a finger into a deep crease around his neck, felt something besides skin, and leaned closer for a look, forcing the crease open. It was cord, the kind used for Venetian blinds, with a knot under his left ear, and the surplus ends had been tucked under his shoulder. I told myself then and there to remember to ask the murderer, when we had him, if he had tucked the cord in consciously because he liked things neat, or if his mind had been occupied and he had done it without thinking. It was one of the most remarkable details I have ever seen or heard of about a death by violence. I was resisting the temptation to pull it out to see how much there was of it when there was a sound behind me, and I twisted around and then sprang up. Sally was there, staring down, her mouth hanging open, and she was starting to sag as I reached her. Not wanting a faint to deal with, I picked her up, carried her to a chair at the other side of the room, put her in it, pushed her head forward, down to her knees, and kept my hand there, at the back of her nice neck. She was limp and there was no resistance, but she wasn't out. I knelt beside her, in case she went.

"So you were wrong," I said, "dead wrong. If you hadn't been wrong you wouldn't have come to Nero Wolfe, but to hell with that now. Do you hear me?"

No answer.

"Damn it, do you hear me?"

"Yes." It wasn't loud, but it was audible. "Is he dead?"

"Certainly he's dead. He—"

"How?"

"Strangled. There's a cord around his throat." I took my hand away, and her head started up, slow, and I stood up. "Do you think you can walk?"

"I don't . . . want to walk." Her head was up.

"That's too bad. Will I have to carry you down and put you in a cab?"

"Archie." Her head tilted back to look up at me. Her jaw started working, out of control, and she stopped to manage it. She made it, and asked, "He killed himself?"

"No. I'll be glad to help you straighten your mind out

later but now I have things to do. He was murdered. I don't want you here when the cops come. I'd rather explain why we came and got Dobbs to let us in without your help. Do you want to spend the night answering questions?"

"No."

"Can you make it down and get a taxi? Mr. Wolfe will be expecting you. I'll phone him."

"I think . . . I'll go home."

"You will not. Absolutely not. Either you give me your word that you'll go straight back there or you stay here and take it. Well?"

"I don't want to stay."

"Will you go to Nero Wolfe and do what he says?"

"Yes."

"Okay. Can you stand? Can you walk?"

She could. I didn't help her. I went to the door and opened it, and she came, none too steady but she made it. Propping the door open with my foot, I reached for the elevator button and pushed it, and when it came and the door opened she entered and pushed the button, and the door closed. I went back in, crossed to a table in a corner where I had seen a phone, lifted the receiver, and dialed the number I knew best.

Wolfe's voice came: "Yes?" He never has answered the phone properly and never will.

"Me," I said. "In Kalmus's apartment. Everything worked fine as planned. Sally did all right, and Superintendent Dobbs brought us up and let us in and left. But Kalmus was here and still is. He's stretched out on the floor with a cord tight around his neck. He has started to cool off, but of course skinny ones cool faster. At a guess, he has been dead around three hours. He didn't tie the cord himself, and anyway the loose ends are neatly tucked under his shoulder."

Silence for five seconds, then: "Pfui."

"Yes, sir. I agree. I have bounced Sally, she just left, and, if she stays conscious and keeps her promise, she will be there in about ten minutes. I have a suggestion. Send her up to bed and have Doc Vollmer come. He may find that she needs a sedative and shouldn't see any callers, official or otherwise, until sometime tomorrow. I'll notify the law right away, since they'll learn from Dobbs what time he let us in. Have you any instructions?"

"No. Confound it."

"Yes, sir. Absolutely. I assume I don't tell the law what we had in mind when we came, since what was in our minds is none of their damned business. You wondered why Kalmus didn't show up this evening, and when I tried his number there was no answer, so we came to ask him. Will that do?"

"Yes. Must you stay?"

"Oh, no. I'm staying because I like it here. Tell Fritz I may be there for breakfast and I may not."

I hung up and took a couple of seconds to shake my head at the phone with my lips tight. Must I stay. Only a genius could ask such a damn fool question. Still shaking my head, I picked up the phone and dialed another number I knew: WA 9-8241. I dialed that instead of Headquarters because I preferred to tell Inspector Cramer himself, or at least Sergeant Purley Stebbins, if either of them was on duty.

11

A couple of electricians had installed a juke box inside my skull, and they were still there, testing it to see how many selections it could play simultaneously. About a dozen, apparently, judging from the noise. Also they were jumping up and down to find out how much vibration it could stand. Or maybe it wasn't a juke box, it was a band, and they were all jumping up and down. If I wanted to see which it was I would have to turn my eyes around to look inside, and in the effort to do that my lids came open, and there facing me was the clock on my bedstand. I quit trying to reverse my eyes and concentrated on the clock. Seventeen minutes past eleven. The noise was neither a juke box nor a band; it was the house phone buzzer. Someone somewhere had a finger on the button and was keeping it there. Nuts. I could stop it by reaching for the cord and yanking it loose. But it takes a hero to do something as sensible as that, and I wasn't awake enough to be a hero, so when I reached I got the phone instead of the cord, brought it to the neighborhood of my mouth, and said, "Now what?"

Wolfe's voice came: "I'm in the kitchen. What time did you get home?"

"Nine minutes to seven, and had three fingers of bourbon while I was fixing a bowl of milk toast. I intended to sleep through until dinner. Why are you in the kitchen?"

"Mr. Cramer is in the office. Have you anything I should know?"

"Yes. Lieutenant Rowcliff's stutter is getting worse. Sergeant Stebbins has a bandage on the middle finger of his left hand, probably got bit by a pigeon he was trying to put salt on the tail of. An assistant DA named Schipple whom I never met before has amended the Constitution; a man is guilty until he proves he's innocent. That's all. In my answers to ten thousand questions and in the statement I signed there was nothing to affect your program if you have one. I didn't even admit in so many words that Sally is your client. As for Kalmus, he was hit on the back of the head, probably with a heavy metal ash tray that was there on a table, before the cord was tied around his throat. The cord was from one of the window blinds there in the room. The ME's on-the-spot guess was that he had been dead two to five hours. Where's Sally?"

"In the south room." (Even after three nights, not "in her room.") "Dr. Vollmer is attending. Before he dosed her last evening I told her why you went to that apartment—when she is asked. How soon can you be down?"

"Oh, six hours. What does Cramer want? He can't want me, he had me off and on all night. Does he want Sally?"

"I don't know. When he arrived I came to the kitchen and Fritz took him to the office. He may presume to quote something you said, even something in your statement, and you should be present. Can you be down in ten minutes?"

"Yes, but I won't. Twenty. Tell Fritz I would appreciate orange juice and coffee."

He said certainly and hung up, and I stretched out on my back and yawned good and wide before reaching to switch the electric blanket off. On my feet, before I closed the open window I stuck my head out for a whiff of winter air, which helped a little, enough to rouse me to the point where I could put my pants on right side front and my shoes on the right feet. More than that couldn't be expected. All night, in between sessions with dicks and the assistant DA, I had considered the situation with Kalmus out of it, and had decided that the best idea would be for the morning mail to bring a letter from Kalmus, telling why he had killed Jerin and saying that after his talk with Wolfe he knew it was all up, so he was bowing out. I might have gone to bed looking forward to the morning mail but for one thing. It wasn't positively inconceivable that he had tied the cord himself, but he simply could not have tucked the ends under his shoulder; he would have been too far gone.

By the time I got downstairs, in twenty minutes flat, my personal fog had cleared a little. In the kitchen, Wolfe, at the center table inspecting a string of dried mushrooms, put it down when I appeared, and moved. I said, "Orange juice," and he said Fritz would bring it, and I sidestepped to let him by, and followed him to the office. If Cramer, in the red leather chair, wished us a good morning he didn't say so. As we went to our desks he looked at his wrist watch, not just a glance but holding his cuff back with his other hand and staring, and as Wolfe sat he rasped, "Half an hour, by God. If you were the Mayor, but you're not."

"I offer no apology," Wolfe said, no hard feeling. "You had no appointment."

Cramer uttered a word that I omit, out of respect for his rank and his long and faithful public service. He was short on sleep too, and his eyes showed it. But he went on, "Appointment my ass. In the kitchen lapping up beer?" His hand went to his inside breast pocket and came out with a piece of paper. "This is to you, but it was found on the body of a man who died by violence, so it's evidence and I'm keeping it. Shall I read it to you?"

Wolfe's shoulders went up an eighth of an inch. "As you please. I would return it."

"When?"

"As soon as Mr. Goodwin makes a copy of it."

Cramer looked at me. Apparently he decided that I would probably eat it, for he shook his head and said, "I'll read it." He unfolded the paper. "Printed at the top is 'From the desk of Daniel Kalmus.' It's dated yesterday, February 14, 1962. It says, written by hand, in ink: 'To Nero Wolfe: I hereby engage your professional services in my behalf and will pay you a reasonable fee plus necessary expenses. My attorney, Daniel Kalmus, will explain what I wish investigated, and

you will work in collaboration with him and at his direction.'
It's signed, 'Matthew Blount.' " He looked at me. "I see you've
got it down."

"Sure," I said, and closed my notebook.

He returned the paper to his pocket. "All right," he told
Wolfe, "I want to know. Monday you announced through
Goodwin that you had been hired on behalf of Blount.
Kalmus denied it. Tuesday you told me you had been hired
but wouldn't say who had hired you. Wednesday, yesterday, Kalmus comes to you and, according to Goodwin, tells
you that he wants to hire you but he has to get Blount's
okay first. Last night Kalmus is murdered, and in his pocket
is this note to you from Blount. I want to know and you're
going to tell me. First, if you were hired Monday who hired
you?"

Wolfe's brows went up. "Didn't Mr. Goodwin tell you?"

"You know damn well he didn't. He told us damn little.
I wanted to hold him as a material witness, but the DA said
no. Who hired you?"

"Isn't it obvious?" Wolfe turned a hand over. "Since she
went there with Mr. Goodwin last evening, and I hadn't yet
been engaged by Mr. Kalmus or Mr. Blount? Surely you can
add two and two. Miss Blount, of course."

Cramer nodded. "Yeah, I can add. Now that you know I
already know, you tell me. I also know she has been here
since Monday night, and she's here now. I want to see her."

"She's under a doctor's care and you must have his permission. Dr. Edwin A. Voll—"

"Nuts. She discovered a dead body and left before the
police arrived. Where is she, in the kitchen?"

"Mr. Goodwin discovered the body and you kept him all
night." Wolfe turned to me. "Tell Miss Blount to bolt the
door."

I swiveled to get the house phone, but Cramer roared,
"Your goddam clowning!" and I swiveled back and grinned at
him, and told Wolfe, "I hate to disturb her. If he starts upstairs there'll be time enough."

"That's the first thing you wanted to know," Wolfe told
Cramer. "Miss Blount was and is my client. Now her father
is too if I accept the engagement. Next?"

Cramer had his fingers curled over the chair arms, re-
gaining control. He must have told himself many times over
the years never to let Wolfe get him roaring, and here he

had done it again. I expected him to get out a cigar and give it a massage, but Fritz saved him the trouble and expense by coming with my orange juice and coffee on a tray, and by the time he had put it on my desk and gone, and I had picked up the glass and taken a sip, Cramer had himself in hand.

He cleared his throat. "You remember," he said, a little hoarse, "that I said Tuesday I knew damn well you hadn't been hired. Okay, maybe I was wrong. But I also said that I thought you had got hold of something, some piece of information or evidence, that you thought would spring Blount, or at least might, and now I'm sure of it. It's a fair guess that you got it from the daughter. You used it to get Kalmus here. You told him what it was, or gave him a good hint, good enough so he told Blount and advised him to hire you, and Blount wrote you this note." He tapped his chest. "But Kalmus went ahead and did something with that piece of information himself without calling you in, and he got himself killed, and you learned about it or suspected it, and when Goodwin went there last night, taking the daughter along to get him in, he *expected* to find a corpse."

He paused for breath. "You and your goddam tricks. You probably *told* Kalmus to try something. I'd bet a dollar to a dime that you know who killed him. All right, you've jockeyed yourself into a fee, and Kalmus is dead, but your client is still in jail. Can you pry him loose or can't you? I'm not going to tell you for the twentieth time that if and when the DA thinks he can get you for obstructing justice by withholding evidence I'll do all I can to make it stick, and it looks as if this is it. Do I have to get a warrant for the arrest of Sarah Blount as a material witness?"

Wolfe, leaning back, took in air, all he had room for, which was plenty, and let it out. "Day before yesterday," he said, "I told you that you were incomparably better acquainted than I was with all the circumstances surrounding the death of Paul Jerin. That was true, and it still is, and it is equally true of the circumstances surrounding the death of Daniel Kalmus. You've had your army working at it for twelve hours, and I have merely read the morning paper. I have had no report from Mr. Goodwin. As for his expecting to find a corpse when he went there last night, at that time he was of the opinion, and so was I, that Kalmus had probably murdered Paul Jerin."

Cramer again uttered a word that I omit, the same one, and this time he added nothing.

"Not an opinion based on evidence," Wolfe said, "only on a suspicion held by a person I had spoken with, now of course discredited. You know Saul Panzer, Fred Durkin, and Orrie Cather."

"I ought to. What about them?"

"I hired them yesterday. Their assignment was to find evidence that Kalmus procured or possessed arsenic in some form prior to Tuesday evening, January thirtieth. When Mr. Panzer telephoned this morning I told him to drop it. Naturally."

Cramer was staring. "That's not your kind of lie. Three men would have to back it up."

"Nor ordinarily, I hope, my kind of truth—admission of error. Two hundred dollars of Miss Blount's money wasted."

Cramer still stared. "Kalmus was Blount's lawyer. You thought *he* had put arsenic in the chocolate? Why?"

"I considered that the most likely alternative. I reserve the *why*; as I said, it wasn't based on evidence. Now for the only alternatives left—Hausman, Yerkes, and Farrow—since Blount is excluded. Don't you too exclude him now? Your elaborate theory of my trickery was at fault, but one of its assumptions, that Kalmus was killed by the man who killed Jerin, is surely sound, and Blount is in jail. Should you keep him there?"

Cramer looked at me. I had the orange juice down and was on the second cup of coffee. "You lied in that statement," he said. "You said you went to Kalmus's place to find out if Blount had okayed hiring Wolfe, and what you really went for was to search it to try to find—" He cut it off short. "Oh, nuts." He got up. "This is the first time I ever left here," he told Wolfe, "thinking you may have grabbed a bear's tail and can't let go. You *may* have. If you actually thought at ten o'clock last night that Kalmus had killed Jerin where are you now? Who comes next? Huh?"

He turned and was on his way, but I stayed put, ready to whirl to the house phone. He just might make a dash for the stairs and the south room, and if I were in the hall it would be ticklish. You can bolt a door on a cop, but you can't touch him. But he turned right, to the front, and when the sound came of the door closing I stepped to the hall to see that he wasn't still inside, then returned to my desk,

poured coffee, emptying the pot, and took a swallow. Wolfe
had his arms folded and his eyes shut. I sat and drank coffee. The morning mail was there on my desk pad, mostly
junk stuff as usual, and, when my cup was empty, I started
slitting it open.

Wolfe's voice came, a growl. "You had four hour's sleep."

"I did. not." I didn't turn. "It takes time to make milk
toast and eat it. Do you want a report?"

"No."

I opened an envelope. "Here's another invitation to be-
come a charter member of the National Foundation for the
Control of Crime. Have you any instructions for me regarding
crime?"

"I have a question. Can you see Mr. Blount today? Now?"

"I doubt it. No one can visit a man in for murder without
bail but his lawyer and members of his immediate family, on
a permit from the DA's office. The visiting hours are from
six to eight P.M. He's your client, but you're not a lawyer.
We can ask the DA's office for an exception and get turned
down. Cramer might fix it as a special personal favor."

"Pfui."

"Check." I opened another envelope and removed the contents. "Weniger has a fresh batch of ready-mixed Berrichon
cheese which is incredibly delicious. When we found Kalmus last night Sally's first idea was to go home to mother.
Are you sure she's in her room?"

"No."

I turned. "No?"

"Fritz took a breakfast tray to her, and Dr. Vollmer came
and saw her shortly before ten o'clock. I was in the plant
rooms as usual, and he spoke to me on the house phone."

"She could have walked downstairs and on out."

"Yes. Go and see."

I swiveled, rose, and headed for the hall. Naturally he
was boiling, since she had given him a bum steer on Kalmus, but the one sure thing was that we had to reach Blount,
and we had a member of his immediate family right there.
Or we had had. On my way down I had noticed that her
door was closed and, mounting two steps at a time, I found
that it still was. I was so sure she had blown that my hand
went to the knob without knocking, but I told it no, and it
swerved and rapped, somewhat louder than necessary; and

her voice came immediately: "Who is it?", and I opened the door and entered.

She was standing over by a window, and even with the light at her back, it was apparent from a glance that she was twenty years older. Since Vollmer had dosed her she must have slept, but she looked a lot worse than I felt with my measly three hours. She had nothing to say, just stood facing me as I approached. I stopped at two arms' length, eyed her, shook my head, and said, "If you'll take some friendly advice, don't look in a mirror. What the hell. You were wrong about him, but you didn't kill him. Fritz and I can give you an air-tight alibi. Inspector Cramer called and one of the things he wanted was to see you, but Mr. Wolfe said no. When one of them does see you, you can come clean with why we went there last night—to look for something that might put it on Kalmus—but when they ask why we suspected him, as they will, just say you don't know, they'll have to ask Mr. Wolfe or me. I came to tell you that and also to see if you were still here. I thought you might have cleared out, gone home. I'm going on talking because it may buck you up to hear the manly voice of one who is still with you all the way in spite of your bobble on Kalmus. If and when you wish to speak raise your hand. Speaking for myself, with only a professional interest, not personal, the silver lining makes up for the cloud. Cramer realizes that if whoever killed Jerin also killed Kalmus, and that's better than even money, he's got the wrong man in the coop. He'll hate to let go, and so will the DA, but your father isn't just riffraff. A suit by him for false arrest would be a lulu. Do you want to say something or shall I go on?"

"Archie," she said.

I nodded. "That's me. That's a good start. You're Sally Blount. Lunch in an hour and a half."

"What will . . . what am I going to do?"

"Snap out of it, of course. You've had a hell of a jolt, and at least you're on your feet, which is something. Fix your hair and get some lipstick on before lunch. I think it very likely that Mr. Wolfe will ask you to go and see your father this afternoon. A note written by him to Nero Wolfe, engaging his services, was found in Kalmus's pocket, and naturally we want—"

The house phone buzzed. In that room it was on a table in a corner, and I went and got it and said, "Me."

Wolfe's voice: "I'm in the kitchen. Is she there?"

"Yes. The worse for wear, but she's here."

She was standing there staring at me.

"Her mother is in the office and wishes to see her. Fritz will bring her up."

"Hold it!" I took two seconds. "No. I'll bring her down. Take it from your expert on females, that's better. I'll explain why some day when you have an hour to spare."

"I would prefer—"

"Sure you would. That's the only chair you really like. A little hardship will be good for you."

I hung up and turned. I considered leading up to it, decided not to bother, and said, "Your mother's downstairs and wants to see you. Lipstick?"

You never know. She might have collapsed, or screamed, or set her jaw and refused to budge, or anything. What she did was say "All right" and head for the door, and as I followed her out and down the two flights I was reminding myself of the one basic rule for experts on females: confine yourself absolutely to explaining why she did what she has already done because that will save the trouble of explaining why she didn't do what you said she would. I even forgot to notice the nice neck and the curves into the shoulders.

Mrs. Blount was in the red leather chair. I suppose the tactful thing would have been for me to join Wolfe in the kitchen, but it was I who had spilled the beans at Sally's request, and I might be able to help with the sweeping up, so I went in part way and stood. Mrs. Blount got up, floated up, and took hold of Sally's arms. That woman unquestionably had witch in her; when she rose from a chair you got the impression that she had no need of muscles, it was some kind of automation that IBM never heard of. She didn't say anything, just took Sally's arms and looked, and damned if I didn't catch myself wishing I was Sally. They were close, nearly touching in front.

Sally's chin was up. "I'll say I'm sorry if you want me to," she said, "but I won't say I was wrong. Archie says I was, but I wasn't. He *was* in love with you, you *must* have known it. Lots of men are, you must know they are. Maybe I was wrong not trusting him about father, and if I was I would tell him I was sorry about that, but I can't now. Do you want me to tell *you* I'm sorry?"

Mrs. Blount was slowly shaking her head. "It doesn't matter," she said. "Of course we're both sorry."

"Yes, I suppose we are."

"Of course. I'm as sorry as you are that you hurt Dan like that. You hurt him terribly." She let go of Sally's arms. "About me, men being in love with me, there's nothing to say. You thought that years ago, you told me so, when you were just a child, and what can I say? You don't remember what I said then."

"Oh yes I do. You said love was really love only when it was returned. I never said you returned it. I never *thought* you did. Not even with Dan Kalmus. And what I did, coming to Nero Wolfe, and leaving that night, that had nothing to do with you, that was just for my father."

"I know it was. But—I'm your mother."

"I'd do it for you too. Mother, I *would*."

"I believe you would. But I hope . . ." Mrs. Blount let it hang. She turned. "Mr. Goodwin, it seems to be your lot to hear our intimate affairs. That evening I didn't shake hands with you because I wouldn't mean it, but I would now." She extended a hand. "If you would."

I moved to take the hand. It was small and firm, and cold. "There's no longer a difference of opinion," I said. "Why not sit down?"

Sally had sat, and where, do you suppose? In the red leather chair. As I moved up one of the yellow ones for her mother I was thinking that jealousy wasn't enough, it was more complicated than that, but Mrs. Blount was speaking. "May I see Nero Wolfe? If he's not too busy?"

I said I'd see, and went. In the kitchen Wolfe was on the stool at the big table, drinking beer and watching Fritz peel shallots. He gave me a frown and asked, "They're bickering?"

"No, sir. They're both sorry, but Sally copped the red leather chair. Mrs. Blount wants to see you if you're not too busy. She shook hands with me, so be prepared for physical contact with a woman."

Nothing doing. He said something to Fritz, left the stool, picked up the glass with one hand and the bottle with the other, proceeded to the office and on in, stopped three paces short of the yellow chair, said, "I'm Nero Wolfe, Mrs. Blount," bowed from the waist like an ambassador or a butler, went to his desk, put the glass and bottle down, sat, and asked Sally, "Should you be up? Dr. Vollmer said you need rest and quiet."

"I'm all right," she said. She didn't look it.

He turned to the mother. "You wanted me?"

She nodded. "Yes. My husband does. He wants you to come—he wants to see you. Today."

Wolfe grunted. "You have spoken with him?"

"No, but Mr. McKinney has. He's the senior partner in the law firm. He saw him this morning. My husband told him that he wouldn't—oh. Perhaps you don't know. Did Mr. Kalmus tell you, before he—did he tell you yesterday that my husband had written to you to engage your services?"

"No."

"He told me, on the phone yesterday afternoon. He said—"

"What time did he phone you?"

"About six o'clock. A little before six."

"Where did he phone from?"

"I don't know. He said he had told my husband that he thought you should be engaged to investigate something, and my husband had written to you. Then this morning—"

"Did Mr. Kalmus say what I was to investigate?"

"He didn't say *what*, just that it was something only he and my husband knew about. Then this morning Mr. McKinney went to see my husband, and—" She stopped, and smiled. It wasn't actually a smile, just a little twist of her lips that it took good eyes to see. "It isn't natural for me," she said, "saying 'my husband, my husband.' Since you're going to . . . I call him Matt. If I may?"

"As you please, madam."

"This morning Mr. McKinney went to see him, to tell him about Dan—Mr. Kalmus, and he said he wants to see you. He wouldn't tell Mr. McKinney what you are to investigate. Mr. McKinney is getting a permit for you from the District Attorney. He wanted to phone you, to ask you to come to see him, but I told him I would rather come to you. I . . . I insisted."

She didn't look like an insister or sound like one, but toughness is as toughness does, and there she was, no red in her eyes and no sag to her jaw, only a few hours after she had heard about Kalmus. But she wasn't cold, though her hand had been; you couldn't possibly look at her and call her cold.

Wolfe had his arms folded. "The permit will have to be for Mr. Goodwin," he said, "since I leave my house only on personal errands. But I need—"

"Matt told Mr. McKinney that he must see *you*."

"Outside this house Mr. Goodwin is me, in effect—if not my alter ego, my vicar. But I need some information from you. I presume it's your opinion that your husband did not kill Paul Jerin."

"Not my opinion. Of course he didn't."

"Have you considered the alternatives?"

"Why . . . yes. Yes, I have."

"Eliminating the two men in the kitchen, the cook and the steward, and on that I accept the conclusion of the police and the District Attorney, one of four men must have put the arsenic in the chocolate. The four messengers. You realize that?"

"Yes."

"That's manifest. But what was the motive? None of them had had any connection or association with Jerin. Therefore I concluded that the purpose was to injure your husband—indeed, to destroy him—and that purpose had apparently been attained. Yesterday my attention was centered on Mr. Kalmus as the most likely of the four. His objective was you. He wanted you, and your husband was in the way. When Mr. Goodwin—"

"That's absurd, Mr. Wolfe. *Absurd.*"

He shook his head. "It still isn't absurd, now that I've seen you. For any man vulnerable to the lure of a woman, and most men are, you would be a singular temptation. Kalmus's death by violence has made the assumption of his guilt untenable, but it hasn't rendered it absurd. Now we have the other three—Hausman, Yerkes, and Farrow, your nephew. By the only acceptable hypothesis left to us, one of them killed both Jerin and Kalmus—Jerin to injure your husband, and Kalmus because he knew or suspected the truth and threatened exposure. When Mr. Goodwin sees your husband he may learn what it is that Kalmus knew, but you are here and I have questions for you; and if you hope to see your husband cleared you will answer with complete candor. Which of those three men had reason to destroy your husband?"

Her eyes were meeting his, straight. "None of them," she said. "Or if they did . . . no. It's impossible."

"Nothing is impossible in the relations between men and women. Your nephew, Morton Farrow. It has been suggested that he calculated that with your husband gone, through you he would be able to take control of the corporation. Is that impossible?"

"It certainly is. I wouldn't give my nephew control of anything whatever, and he knows it." Again the little twist of her lips. "He came to see you, didn't he?"

"Yes."

"Well?"

Wolfe nodded. "Quite. But it's still possible that he miscalculated. Mr. Hausman?"

She made a little gesture. "Ernst Hausman is Matt's oldest friend. He is our daughter's godfather. He would do anything for Matt, anything. I'm absolutely sure."

"He's a dotard. Just short of demented. He came Monday evening to propose a scheme to extricate your husband unequaled, in my experience, for folly and fatuity. Either he's unhinged or he's exceptionally crafty, and if the latter you have been hoodwinked. Mr. Yerkes?"

She shook her head. "No."

"Your daughter got him to come here, and he told me himself of dissension with your husband. He wants to be president of his bank, and your husband favors another candidate."

She nodded. "I know. Matt has told me. Mr. Yerkes knows why, and he doesn't resent it. It hasn't affected their friendship."

"Pfui. Are they paragons? But granting that, even a paragon is still a man. If it wasn't absurd to suppose that Mr. Kalmus coveted you, what about Mr. Yerkes? He has seen much of you, hasn't he?"

For five seconds I thought she wasn't going to reply. She sat stiff, her eyes level at him. Then she said, "Must you go out of your way to be offensive, Mr. Wolfe?"

"Nonsense," he snapped. "Offensive to whom? I suggest that you have a person and a personality capable of arousing desire; should that offend you? I suggest that Mr. Yerkes is

not blind and has sensibility; should that offend him? We
are not tittle-tattling, madam; we are considering your husband's fate. I asked for candor. How does Mr. Yerkes feel
toward you?"

"We are friends." She stayed stiff. "But only because he
and my husband are friends. My daughter has given you a
wrong impression." She turned to the daughter. "I'm not
blaming you, Sally, but you have." Back to Wolfe. "If you
didn't mean to offend . . . very well. But I'm just what I
am, a middle-aged woman, and what you suggest, I can't believe it. I certainly can't believe it of Charles Yerkes."

Obviously she meant every word. Lon Cohen had been
right, she simply didn't know it. Wolfe's eyes were narrowed at her. The minute we were alone he would ask his
expert on females for the low-down on her, and the expert
was ready.

"Then we've wasted ten minutes," he said. He looked up
at the wall clock. "What is to be done, what *can* be done,
now depends on what Mr. Goodwin learns from your husband, and speculation on that would be idle. Can you reach
Mr. McKinney now? To tell him that the permit must be
for Mr. Goodwin?"

"Yes. At his office. He said he would be there."

"Do you know his number?"

She said she did, and floated up, and I vacated my chair
for her; and she came and took it and dialed. My eyes went
to Sally, and the look she gave me said as plain as words,
And now of course you've fallen for her too. Which was a
lie. I merely agreed with Wolfe that she had a person and a
personality capable of arousing desire, a purely objective
judgment.

12

At a quarter to five that afternoon I was seated on a wooden chair at a wooden table, face to face with Matthew Blount, with my notebook on the table and my pen in my hand. After years of practice I had proved more than once that I could report verbatim, without notes, an hour-long three- or four-way conversation, but I was taking no chances with this one. Once before, six years back, I had been admitted to the hoosegow to confer with a man in for the big one, by name Paul Herold, alias Peter Hays, but that time there had been a grill between us, in a big room which contained other inmates and visitors. This time the room was small and we had no company; the guard who had brought him was standing outside the glass door. Of course there were two reasons why the DA had let me come at an off hour and given us some privacy: one, Blount was a prominent citizen with plenty of prominent friends; and two, the murder of Kalmus had made him suspect that he had hold of the short end of the stick.

Matthew Blount, forty-seven, Harvard 1937, did not look as you would expect of a man who had been in the jug for twelve days on a murder rap. Not that he was chipper, but the skin of his well-arranged face, shaved that day, was smooth and clear, his hair had been trimmed within three or four days, his hands were perfectly clean and so were his nails, his custom-made jacket might have been pressed that morning, his shirt was on its first day, and he had a necktie on. He could have gone as was to Peacock Alley for a drink if he could have got past the guard at the door and on out.

It wasn't easy to persuade him that I was as good as Nero Wolfe. I explained that even if Wolfe had broken the one rule he never broke, and come, it wouldn't have made any difference, because as soon as he got home he would have told me everything that was worth telling.

"No, he wouldn't," Blount said. "He would have been bound to secrecy."

"Not a chance," I said. "No one has ever bound him to secrecy or ever will if it means leaving me out. He leaves me out only if and when *he* wants to. If he had come and you insisted that he keep it strictly to himself he would have walked out on you."

He shook his head. "I have told this to no one, not even my wife, because I was ashamed of it. I still am. Only Kalmus knew about it, and he's dead. I don't—oh. You're Archie Goodwin? You went there and found him, and my daughter was with you?"

"Right."

"Did my daughter—how was she?"

"She did fine. Three minutes after we found him she could leave on her own feet, alone, take the elevator down, and get a taxi. Your wife and daughter are both fine, as I told you, Mr. Blount. As soon as—"

"Forget the Mister."

"Sure. As soon as it had been arranged for me to get the permit to see you they left together, for home."

"I want a straight answer to a straight question. Did my wife tell Wolfe what it is that I want him to investigate?"

"No. She said she didn't know. She said no one knew—except Kalmus."

He nodded. "Then he kept his word. There aren't many men you can rely on absolutely. Dan Kalmus was one. And he's dead." He set his jaw. In a moment he went on, "This thing I'm ashamed of, I have told no one. McKinney wanted me to tell him this morning, he insisted, but I wouldn't. I didn't tell Kalmus, he knew all about it. From what he told me about Nero Wolfe, I decided he was the man to tell. Now you say I must tell you."

"Not you must. I only say that telling me is the same as telling Mr. Wolfe. I add this, that I will tell only him. Also I'll tell you what he would say if you tried to bind him to secrecy. He would say that the best protection for your secret would be his discretion, and that if a circumstance arose that made him think it necessary to disclose it he would first tell you. That's the best you'd get from him. From me, you get my word that I'll tell him and no one else in any circumstances whatever."

Our eyes were meeting, and he knew how to meet eyes. "Kalmus was my lawyer," he said.

"I know he was."

"Now I'll have to get another one, and I won't tell him, and I won't want you or Wolfe to tell him."

"Then we won't. What the hell, Blount, what is it? After all this—did you poison that chocolate yourself?"

"Yes. I did."

I stared. "*You* did?"

"Yes."

"Then no wonder." I put the pen in my pocket and closed the notebook, which I hadn't used. For this I preferred my memory to a notebook, which could be lost or even possibly taken from me on my way out. I demanded, "This is the fact known only to Kalmus and you that he was counting on to clear you?"

"Yes. I bitterly regret it and I'm bitterly ashamed of it. As you know, I made the arrangements for Jerin to come to the club. I arranged all the details. I knew he drank chocolate when he was playing chess, and I told the steward to have some prepared. I don't know, and I never will know, how in the name of God I conceived the idea of putting something in the chocolate that would befuddle him. I'm not a practical joker, I never have been. It may have been suggested by something somebody said, but if so I don't remember it, and anyway it was I who did it. It's even possible that I was prouder of my skill at chess than I thought I was and I had a subconscious resentment of a man who could give me odds of a rook and beat me. I hate to think I'm that petty, but damn it, I did it. I put something in the chocolate while I was taking it upstairs and stirred it with a pencil."

"Arsenic, to befuddle him?"

"It wasn't arsenic. It was poison, since anything toxic is a poison, but it wasn't arsenic. I didn't know exactly what it was until later, when I had it analyzed. Kalmus got it for me. I told him what I intended to do, as a precaution; there wasn't much risk of discovery, but I wanted to know if it would be criminally actionable. He said no, and he liked the idea, and that wasn't surprising because I thought he would, it was the kind of prank that would appeal to him. But he said I must be extremely careful of what I used, of course I knew that, and he offered to find out what would be best for the effect we wanted, and I asked him to get it, and he said he would. Which he did. He gave it to me that evening, that Tuesday evening, at the club. It was a two-ounce bottle, a liquid, and he told me to use about half of it. Which I did." He pointed a finger at me. "Listen, Goodwin. I don't want my wife or daughter ever to know what an incredible chump I was, in *any* circumstances."

"Yeah. I don't blame you. So of course you had to go for the chocolate and take it to him."

"Of course."

"And when Yerkes came and told you Jerin was sick you went and got the pot and cup and washed them out and brought fresh chocolate."

"Of course. I went to see him, and obviously he had had enough."

"Did you suspect then that there was something in the chocolate besides what you put in?"

"No, why should I? Kalmus had given me the bottle, and it had been in my pocket until I used it."

"When he got worse and Kalmus got Dr. Avery to go to him, didn't you suspect *then* that something else had been put in the chocolate by someone?"

"No. I didn't suspect that until two days later, Thursday. What I did suspect was that a mistake had been made in preparing the contents of the bottle. So did Kalmus. I began to suspect that when Jerin got so bad he had to be taken to the hospital, and on my way to the hospital—I walked, and I was alone—I hid the bottle, and later, on my way home—"

"Where did you hide it?"

"In a plant tub. In the areaway of one of the houses I passed there was a tub with an evergreen shrub, and I put the bottle in under the peat moss. When I left the hospital later, that was after Jerin died, I got it and took it home, and the next day I took it to a laboratory to have it analyzed. I got the report—"

"What laboratory?"

"The Ludlow Laboratories on Forty-third Street. I got the report on the analysis the next day, Thursday, and showed it to Kalmus. It was just what he had ordered, a very mild dilution of a mixture of chloral hydrate and carbon tetra-chloride. It couldn't possibly have been fatal even if I had used all of it."

"No arsenic?"

"No, damn it, just what I said."

"Where's the report now?"

"In a locked drawer in my desk at my office, and the bottle too, with what's left in it."

"Well." I took a moment to look at it. "You didn't *suspect* that someone else had put arsenic in the chocolate, you *knew* it. Didn't you? Since you knew they had found arsenic in Jerin?"

"Of course I knew it."

"Did you have any idea who?"

"No."

"Have you any idea now?"

"Apparently it must have been one of four men, the four who acted as messengers, because they were the only ones who entered the library. That didn't seem possible because none of them could have had any reason. Then last week Kalmus had the idea that the purpose had been to get me —to get me where I am. But who? Of course not Kalmus, and which one of the other three could possibly have wanted to get me? They're my *friends*. One of them is my wife's nephew."

"Are you telling me you still have no idea which one it was?"

"I am."

I turned a hand over. "Look. Last night Kalmus was murdered, and almost certainly by the man who killed Jerin to get you. If so Kalmus had an idea, and a damn good one— too good. He tried to do something about it, which wasn't very bright since he had got you to hire Nero Wolfe, and he got slugged and strangled. He came yesterday afternoon and talked you into hiring Nero Wolfe, didn't he?"

"He didn't have to talk me into it. I didn't oppose it."

"But he talked, and he had some one man in mind. He must have. Didn't he say who?"

"No. He only said that he would have to tell Nero Wolfe about it, about what I had put in the chocolate, because he had to have an expert investigator and Wolfe was the best. If he had any one man in mind he didn't say so. He just— wait a minute. He did say one thing. He asked me if I didn't see what might have happened, and I said no and asked him what he meant, and he said he would tell me after he had discussed it with Wolfe. You think he had a particular man in mind?"

"Of course he did."

"Who?"

That was one of the biggest temptations I have ever had to strangle. It would have been highly satisfying to show the client then and there that while Wolfe had the best brain he didn't have the only brain, not to mention the additional pleasure of telling Wolfe what I had told the client. But I had to skip it; there was one chance in a thousand that I was wrong, and I needed to examine it for possible holes.

So I shook my head. "Search me," I said. "There may have been something in his apartment that would give a hint, but if so the cops have got it now. I could go on asking you questions, plenty of them, but I've got what I came for, the fact that was known only to Kalmus and you, and it's quite a fact, and Kalmus would be alive now if he had waited to consult Nero Wolfe instead of going ahead on his own." I picked up the notebook that had nothing in it. "When Mr. Wolfe decides how to proceed he may let you know and he may not. With you here it's complicated and it takes time." I rose and got my hat and coat from a chair. "He can't consult with your lawyer because even if you had one you wouldn't want him to know about this."

"But how will he—what will he do?"

"I don't know. That's for him. One thing sure, he'll do something, but first he may send me back to you with questions. You may see me again tomorrow." I stuck an arm in the coat.

He was on his feet. "My God," he said. "My whole—I'm completely in the hands of a man I've never seen. Remember what I said, I'd rather stay here a month, a year, than have my wife and daughter know what an utter fool I was."

That was what was on his mind as we parted, with a handshake, but not on mine. Was it possible that it was as simple as it looked? Wasn't there a catch somewhere? As I went along the corridor, under escort, and on out to the sidewalk, and flagged a taxi, I looked it over from every angle, and by the time the taxi turned into Thirty-fifth Street I had decided that it was a hundred to one on two conclusions: one, I knew exactly what had happened that evening at the Gambit Club; and two, it would take a better man than even Nero Wolfe to prove it. There was positively no crack anywhere to get a wedge started.

But at least I could jostle him. Whatever he might have

expected me to bring back, if anything, he hadn't expected
this. It was two minutes past six as the taxi rolled to the
curb in front of the old brownstone, so he would be down
from the plant rooms. I paid the hackie and got out, mounted
the stoop and used my key, put my hat and coat on the hall
rack, and went to the office. He was at his desk, opening a
book with a blue binding; apparently *African Genesis* was
finished. As I crossed to my desk he closed it. I put the
unused notebook in the drawer, sat and faced him, and said,
"I can name the man who killed Paul Jerin and Dan Kalmus."

"Flummery," he growled.

"No, sir. Any odds you name. But I prefer to see if you're
as sharp as I am, so I'll just report, and I'll begin by giving
you the jolt Blount gave me. He poisoned the chocolate."

"Pfui. Who killed Kalmus?"

"You'll soon know. Verbatim?"

"Yes."

I gave it to him, straight through. Usually he closes his
eyes when I start a report and keeps them closed, but that
time they opened when I asked Blount if he had poisoned
the chocolate himself and he said yes, he did, and they didn't
close again until Blount said the report and the bottle were
in a drawer in his office desk. When I finished he opened
them, cocked his head, and said, "No wonder you can name
him."

"Yes, sir. I guess it's a tie. I have a question. Had this possibility occurred to you Tuesday noon when you had Sally
phone and get them to come, including him?"

"No. How could it? It was the chocolate that made Jerin
ill, indubitably. Now that is accounted for." He took a deep
breath. "I am inexpressibly relieved. It has been all but in-
tolerable, the strain of insulting my intelligence by forcing
it to assume that one of them tampered with the chocolate
when he entered to report a move, with Jerin there, and with
the likelihood—no, certainty—that someone would interrupt
at any instant. I knew it was egregious, and so did you.
This is satisfactory, Archie." He breathed deep again. "An
analeptic for my self-esteem. Has it any flaws?"

That showed how hard he had been taking it, asking me
if it had any flaws instead of telling me. As I reported he
had been so busy enjoying the feel of the pressure going

that he hadn't concentrated, though he had got the main point.

"None that I can see," I said. "Of course his killing Kalmus is what settles it. With Kalmus and Blount out, and with your inexpressible relief that we can forget the other three messengers, what else is there? The arsenic got in him somehow. Of course there's plenty to guess about, for instance what Kalmus said or did that told him that Kalmus had figured it out, but that's not a flaw, it's only a gap. The only flaw I see is that there's no possible way you can ever prove that he killed Jerin. He's absolutely airtight. On Kalmus there may be a chance. He goes to Kalmus's apartment, maybe invited and expected, maybe not. Anyhow Kalmus lets him in, no doorman or hallman, and the elevator is do-it-yourself. He catches Kalmus off guard, knocks him out with the ash tray, gets the cord and uses it, and leaves. Fingerprints were no problem; they're no problem any more for anyone with an ounce of brains. The only chance would be if someone saw him enter or leave, and naturally the cops are working on that, though not with him in mind. In order to get motive you'd have to prove that he killed Jerin and Kalmus knew it or suspected it, and that's hopeless. As for his motive for killing Jerin, why not your theory, to get Blount because he wanted his wife. He had had more contacts with her person and personality than any of the others. As for taking some arsenic with him when he went to the club that night, that's easy. He knew what Blount was going to do because Kalmus had asked him what to use to get the effect Blount wanted. He would be the natural one for Kalmus to ask."

I nodded. "Perfect. Not a flaw except the one little detail that you and Homicide and the FBI all put together will never hang it on him. He was a sap to kill Kalmus because they might possibly tag him for that if they find someone who saw him enter or leave, and no matter how well Kalmus had it mapped, his killing Jerin, he couldn't possibly have had any evidence to back it up. There just couldn't be any. He could have told Kalmus to go soak his head."

Wolfe grunted. "An adequate exposition."

"I like it."

"Adequate as far as it goes. But granting that Kalmus had no evidence that would convince the police, even if he revealed the fact that Blount was determined to keep secret, his knowledge or suspicion presented another threat. What if he convinced Blount? Or, more to the point, Mrs. Blount?"

I raised a brow. "Yeah. Sure. That would have been a nuisance, no matter what happened to Blount. But while that may explain why he killed Kalmus, it doesn't alter the main—"

I stopped. He had leaned back and closed his eyes and started his lips going, out and in, out and in. As I said before, the lip exercise is not to be interrupted, and I crossed my legs and got comfortable for a two-minute wait, maybe three, glancing at my watch.

It was nearer thirty than three. Twenty-one minutes and ten seconds had passed when he opened his eyes and straightened up, setting a record. As always, I had exercised my mind by trying to decide where and what he was headed for, and as usual, I ended up with an assortment of possibilities, worth a dime a dozen. What he did that time was not in my assortment. No wonder he had taken a while to make up his mind; he had decided he had to call a woman on the phone.

"I must speak with Mrs. Blount," he said. "What's her number?"

I swiveled and reached for the phone, but he snapped, "No. The number. I'll dial it. You aren't here."

I turned. "Where am I?"

"I don't know. You have been dismissed, discharged by me for dereliction of duty immediately after you reported to me on your conversation with Mr. Blount. Don't leave the house. Don't answer the telephone or doorbell. Tell Fritz that if anyone asks for you, you have gone out—that's all he knows. I'll give you instructions after I have spoken with Mrs. Blount. What's her number?"

I told him, and sat and watched him dial it. As I said, that had not been in my assortment, getting fired just after I had brought him inexpressible relief.

13

Three hours later, at twenty minutes to ten, I stood in the alcove at the end of the hall next to the kitchen, observing, through the hole in the wall, the cast that had been assembled for what I consider one of the best charades Wolfe has ever staged.

On the office side the hole is covered by a pretty picture of a waterfall on the wall five feet to the right of Wolfe's desk. On the alcove side it is covered by a metal panel at eye level which slides open without a hint of a noise, and, standing there, you find that the made-to-order waterfall is no obstruction to your view of the office or to your hearing. It wasn't quite as clear for either my eyes or my ears as if I had been inside seated at my desk, but I couldn't very well be there since I had been fired in disgrace, and besides, that chair won't hold two and Saul Panzer was in it.

At twenty minutes to ten Wolfe entered, crossed to his desk, greeted them with three stingy nods—left, center, and right—and sat. All of them except Saul had come at the request of Mrs. Blount, after Wolfe's phone call to her. She had been put in the red leather chair by Saul, as instructed by me. In the front row of yellow chairs Sally was on the left, Ernst Hausman in the center, and Dr. Avery on the right, next to Saul at my desk. Behind them were Morton Farrow, the nephew, and Charles W. Yerkes, the banker.

Sally was the only one who had any idea what was up. Because she had had to be not only briefed, but rehearsed, thoroughly, she had come at seven-thirty and eaten dinner with me in the kitchen. In the kitchen for two reasons: so Wolfe could stick to his rule of no business at the table, and so Fritz could hear us. One of them might possibly ask Fritz some question when he admitted them, a question that must be answered right, and he had to know what to say. The one thing Sally didn't know was that I would be watching the performance through the hole. That was no part of it anyway; I was watching only to pass the time and to see and hear Wolfe tell a pack of lies; and Sally would probably have glanced so often at the picture of the waterfall that she might have attracted attention, and Wolfe wanted all the attention.

He was getting it, from seven pairs of eyes. "I don't thank you for coming," he told them, "because you came to oblige Mrs. Blount, not me, and because I am not in a mood to feel gratitude for anything whatever. As you all know, three days ago, Monday, I was hired by Miss Blount to act in the interest of her father. Yesterday he himself wrote me a note engaging my services, though I didn't learn of it until this morning. I am now compelled to make an extremely humiliating admission, and I felt that I should make it to all of you—you who because of your concern have been good enough to come to see me and answer my questions. True, one of you is twice a murderer, one of you killed both Paul Jerin and Daniel Kalmus, but I couldn't exclude him because I can't name him. I won't keep you long. I merely—"

"That's slander," Hausman blurted. "That's libel." His lips parted to show his teeth. "Unless you can prove it. Can you prove it?"

"No." I had Wolfe in profile and couldn't see his eyes. "Nor do I expect to. I am withdrawing from the case. I shall return to Miss Blount the fee she paid me. I have received none from her father."

I can't report the reactions of the others because I was focused on Sally. She did fine. She stared, and her mouth dropped open, and then she jumped up and cried, "But you can't! You *can't!* Where's Archie?" I could report on Mrs. Blount if there were anything to report, since her profile was almost on the line to Sally, but she didn't move or speak.

"Sit down," Wolfe commanded the former client. "Confound it, don't interrupt. This is the most galling moment of my long experience, and I don't want to prolong it. Mr. Goodwin is not here and he will never be here. I owe this—"

"Why? Where is he?"

"I don't know. Sit down! If you want him try Gehenna; if he isn't there he should be. I owe this to him." Wolfe's head turned to Mrs. Blount. "I force myself to face you, madam. I told you today that yesterday my attention was centered on Mr. Kalmus, but I didn't tell you what I had done about

it. Yesterday afternoon I put four men to work. One of them
is present, at the desk that was Mr. Goodwin's—Mr. Saul
Panzer. Two of them were given certain errands pertaining
to Mr. Kalmus. The other two, Mr. Panzer and Mr. Goodwin,
were told to keep Mr. Kalmus under constant surveillance,
dividing the hours. Late in the afternoon, by an unavoidable
mischance, Mr. Panzer lost contact, and when he phoned to
report it—" He turned. "What time, Saul?"

"Five-thirty-nine," Saul said.

Wolfe turned back. "Mr. Goodwin told him he would meet
him at Mr. Kalmus's house and would take over for the
evening. They met there a few minutes after six, and Mr.
Panzer quit for the day, and Mr. Goodwin found a suitable
post for watching the entrance to the house. Of course the
one inviolable rule for such a job is that the surveillance
must be constant. Otherwise—"

"But I don't understand." Mrs. Blount turned to Sally.
"You went there with him—Mr. Goodwin. You told me you
left at ten o'clock."

That had been deliberately invited. That point had to
be covered. Not only did millions of people, all who read
murder news in the papers, know that Sally and I had entered the house together, and when, but also Sally had told
me that she had told her mother that she had eaten dinner
with Wolfe and me Wednesday evening. We had considered
briefing and rehearsing Mrs. Blount along with Sally, but
had vetoed it as too risky. It wasn't at all certain that Mrs.
Blount would play, and even if she would she might flub it.
And the point had to be covered.

Sally handled it perfectly. "I know I did," she told her
mother, not apologizing. "But I met him there. I didn't want
to tell you I went alone, to meet him and get Dobbs to let
him into Dan's apartment. I guess I—I was ashamed to. If he
took me, if he made me go . . . that was different." She
jerked her head to Wolfe. "Mr. Wolfe, where is he?"

Wolfe ignored her. "I was saying," he told Mrs. Blount,
"that the surveillance must be constant, for otherwise its
whole purpose may be nullified. Mr. Goodwin knew that,
of course. But during the time he was at his post, or supposed to be, a man he should have recognized, since it was
one of those now in this room, entered that house, and later
he left it, and Mr. Goodwin did not see him. That was in-
excusable nonfeasance, and this morning, when he returned

from a night with the police and the District Attorney, I took him severely to task. But this afternoon, when he returned from his interview with your husband, I learned that it was worse than nonfeasance. He admitted that he had been absent from his post for nearly an hour. He refused to say where he had gone, but that was immaterial. If he had performed his duty, if he had not betrayed my trust, I would know who killed both Jerin and Kalmus, and I could complete the job both your daughter and your husband hired me for."

His head turned to the right and back to the left. "I would know which one of you is a treacherous friend and twice a murderer, and I could proceed with assurance. Now I can't proceed at all. As for Jerin, the chance of finding any cogent evidence is so remote that it's hopeless; and as for Kalmus, if any evidence exists it will be found by the normal police routine, not by me. So I am withdrawing. This is the greatest humiliation I have ever had to suffer, and I felt that all of you should hear me acknowledge it. I owed you that, but not more than that, and I'll leave." He pushed his chair back and rose. "As I said, I have discharged Goodwin, and I intend to see that he loses his license to function as a private detective. Pfui. He is not fit to function as anything whatever." He took a step. "Miss Blount, Mr. Panzer has a check for you, for the amount you paid me. . . . Saul, give it to her." He headed for the door.

Again I can't report reactions, and certainly not words, for I was concentrating on the man I expected to be speaking with in an hour or so, Dr. Avery. He handled his act fully as well as Sally had handled hers. As Wolfe marched out he got up and went to Mrs. Blount and bent over her and spoke, but others were speaking too and I couldn't hear what he said; and when Hausman joined them he gave him place and a minute later went to Sally; and that was when I clamped my teeth, when Avery took hold of Sally's arm. She would pull back or tighten up when he touched her, but by gum she didn't, and she managed her face as if she had been training it for years. Wonderful. Saul rescued her by coming with the check, and she could turn away to say she didn't want to take it, but she finally did, since that was in the script. As she was putting it in her bag I slid the panel shut and beat it to the kitchen. There was one chance in a million that when they left the office one of them would turn left instead of right, and round the corner to the alcove and bump into me, and that would have been regrettable. In the kitchen I went to the refrigerator for a carton of milk, and poured a glass. My part was to come, and I needed some support. Fritz was out in the hall to help Saul speed the parting guests.

I could hear the sounds of their going, including, twice, the closing of the front door, but I stayed put even after Fritz came and told me the coast was clear. A couple of minutes later Saul stepped in, stopped, and stared at me, and demanded, "What are you doing here? This is your day of infamy, and anyway I like my new job. Fritz, help me bounce him."

"Bah," I said. "I could take both of you with one hand. She did all right, huh?"

"She sure did. So did he."

"Why not? He's had plenty of practice. You were magnificent. The way you said *five-thirty-nine*—that was the high point." I went to the house phone and pushed the button for Wolfe's room, and his voice came: "Yes?"

"They're gone, and I'm off. Any changes?"

"No. Proceed."

"Okay. I'll try not to betray your trust again." I hung up, got my coat and hat from the chair where they were waiting and put them on, picked up my luggage, a packed bag also there waiting, told Saul he would hear from me soon, I hoped, and left by the back door. The subject might have turned his ankle going down the steps and be sitting out front rubbing it. The back door leads to the small yard where Fritz grows herbs, or tries to, and at the far end there is a bolted door in the eight-foot fence. Fritz came along to bolt the door after me. A narrow passage between two buildings takes you to Thirty-fourth Street. It was a quarter past ten when I climbed into a taxi and told the hackie the Talbott Hotel, where I had a reservation, and it was a quarter to eleven when, in Room 914, having let the bellhop hang up my coat and tipped him and told him good night, I went to the telephone and asked the switchboard to get a certain number.

One of the million little things you get on to that you'll probably never have any use for but you never know is how to tell the voice of an answering service filly from a maid or secretary. It would take a page to explain so I'll skip it. Since

Dr. Avery was a bachelor there was no question of a wife or daughter. What I got was an answering service, and she said Dr. Avery wasn't available but she would be in touch with him later and did I care to leave a message. I did. I gave her my name and number and room number and said I had to speak with Avery as soon as possible on an extremely urgent matter.

Answering services are often a damned nuisance. If you ring a number and get no answer you can keep trying, but when you get an answering service all you can do is wait, and you don't know if your message will be relayed; and if you keep ringing back, say every ten minutes, she gets sore and you can give odds that it *won't* be relayed. That time, though, I had no kick coming. I had decided to start fidgeting at a quarter to twelve and to get the number again at midnight, so I was at ease in a chair with the *Gazette* when the phone rang at 11:20. I went and got it and told it hello.

"Who is this?" a voice demanded.

A question in that tone doesn't deserve an answer, so I said, "Who wants to know?"

"I'm Victor Avery. Are you Archie Goodwin?"

"Right. I need to be sure it's you, doctor, as much for your protection as for mine. You may remember that Tuesday evening you told Nero Wolfe the name of the gambit you used against Paul Jerin. What was it—the gambit?"

Brief silence. "The Albin Counter Gambit."

"Okay. Is there any chance that anyone is on an extension at your end?"

"No."

"I want to see you. It's a long story, and I'll just sketch it. I am no longer with Nero Wolfe. He fired me this afternoon. At six o'clock yesterday afternoon he sent me to put my eye on the entrance to Daniel Kalmus's house and keep it there. When I reported to him this morning, after spending the night with the cops, I told him that I had seen no one enter or leave that I recognized. This afternoon he tore into me and made me admit that I had been away from my post for about an hour. So he gave me the boot."

"That's unfortunate."

"Yeah. But the point is, I lied to him. I wasn't away from my post. I was right there all evening, and I did see someone

I recognized, entering and leaving. That's what I want to discuss with you."

"Why with me?"

"Well, you've had a lot of experience giving people advice. Doctors get asked about all sorts of things. I think I can get my job back if I go to Mr. Wolfe and tell him the truth, and I want to know if you would advise me to do that. I can't put it off; if I do it at all I'll have to do it tomorrow. So I'll have to see you—say around noon? One o'clock?"

A longer silence. Then, and he managed his voice darned well: "I don't believe a word of this. It's some kind of clumsy trick. I'll have nothing to do with it."

"Okay. I'm sorry, but of course you'll be sorrier than I am. Good night and pleasant dreams."

I hung up, glanced at my watch, and went back to the chair and the paper. The only question was how long it would be. Half an hour? No. In exactly eighteen minutes the phone rang, and when I went and told it hello his voice came: "Goodwin?"

"Speaking. Who is this?"

"Victor Avery. On second thought I have decided I may be able to give you some good advice. Not at noon or one o'clock because I have appointments. The fact is, it would be difficult for me to make it before evening, around seven o'clock. The best place for a private conversation is in a car, and we can use mine. I'll pick you up at some convenient—"

"Save it," I cut in. It was time to get tough. "Do you think you're dealing with a cluck? Listen, and get it. There's a little restaurant, Piotti's, P-i-o-t-t-i, on Thirteenth Street just east of Second Avenue, downtown side. I'll be there, inside, expecting you, at one o'clock tomorrow. If you're not there by one-fifteen I'll go straight to Nero Wolfe. And I'll go anyway if you don't have with you one hundred thousand dollars in cash. Good night again."

"Wait! That's fantastic! I couldn't possibly get any such amount. And why should I?"

"Forget the rhetoric. Bring as much as you can, and don't make it peanuts, and maybe we can arrange about the rest. Now I'm going to bed and I don't like to be disturbed. You have it? Piotti, Thirteenth Street east of Second Avenue?"

"Yes."

"Better write it down."

I hung up, straightened, and had a good stretch and yawn. On the whole I thought I had done about as well as Sally, but of course my part wasn't finished. After another stretch I returned to the phone and asked the switchboard to get a number, and in a minute a voice came: "Nero Wolfe's residence, Saul Panzer speaking."

I falsettoed. "This is Liz Taylor. May I please speak to Archie?"

"Archie is out streetwalking, Miss Taylor. I'm just as good, in fact better."

I normalized. "You are like hell. All set. One o'clock at Piotti's. We'll have a busy morning. Meet me for breakfast at eight o'clock in the Talbott restaurant."

"No snags?"

"Not a snag. Like falling off a log. As I said to the subject, pleasant dreams."

Getting ready for bed, as I buttoned my pajama jacket it occurred to me that the character who had done such a neat job with Kalmus might be capable of something really fancy, so after bolting the door I put the table against it and a chair on top. The windows were absolutely inaccessible without a rope down from the roof, and if he could manage that between midnight and seven A.M. he was welcome to me.

14

At ten minutes to one Friday afternoon I was seated at one of the small tables along the right wall of Piotti's little restaurant, eating spaghetti with anchovy sauce and sipping red wine—and not the wine you'll get if you go there. Wolfe had once got John Piotti out of a difficulty and hadn't soaked him, and one result was that whenever I dropped in for a plate of the best spaghetti in New York I got, for sixty cents, a pint of the wine which John reserved for himself and three or four favorite customers, and which was somewhat better than what you paid eight bucks for at the Flamingo. Another result had been that back in 1958 John had let us use his premises for a setup for a trap, including running some wires through the cellar, coming up through the floor in the kitchen at one end, and up to one of the tables in the restaurant at the other end. That was the table I was sitting at.

The morning hadn't been as busy as I had expected, chiefly because the wires running through the cellar were still there, intact, and when we tested them they were as good as new. We didn't have to call in a technician at all. For the kitchen end Saul brought the tape recorder from the cupboard in Wolfe's kitchen, and for the restaurant end I bought the latest model midget mike. That was the main cash outlay, $112.50 for the mike, a lot of lettuce for a mike, but it had to be good and it had to fit into the bowl of artificial flowers on the table. Of course the bowl had to be the same as those on the other tables, and we had a devil of a time making a hole in the bottom for the wires to come through. Against the risk that my table companion would take it into his head to move the bowl and find himself pulling wires up through a hole in the table, which would have stopped the show, we made two smaller holes in the bottom of the bowl and screwed it to the table. So if he tried to move it and it wouldn't budge I could say, "By golly, Piotti doesn't let the customers walk out with anything, does he?"

Everything was in order by half past eleven, well before the lunch hour, which is early in that neighborhood. Saul went to the kitchen, to stick there, since it was just possible that the subject might come for a look around in advance, and it wouldn't do for him to catch sight of the man who had taken my job. I went to the Talbott, to learn if there were any messages for me. There weren't. I phoned Wolfe that we were ready, and returned to Piotti's at twelve-thirty. John had kept the table free, and I took it and began on the spaghetti and wine. At ten minutes to one the tables were pretty well filled with customers, and two of them were known to me. At the next table in front of me, seated facing me, was Fred Durkin, and at the next table but one back of me was Orrie Cather. I was facing the door. Very neat.

At four minutes to one Dr. Victor Avery entered, stopped three steps in, saw my raised hand, and came. I took in a forkload of spaghetti while he removed his coat and hat and hung them on the wall hooks, and I was sipping wine as he sat. He looked more middle-aged than he had last night, more than middle-aged, and not so well-fed.

"The spaghetti here is something special," I said. "Better have some."

He shook his head. "I'm not hungry."

"The wine is special too."

"I never drink during the day."

"Neither do I usually, but this is a special occasion." My eyes were on my plate, where I was twisting spaghetti onto my fork, and I raised them and aimed them at him. "How much did you bring?"

His hands were open on the table and his finger tips were working. "I came out of curiosity," he said. "What kind of a trick is this?" He was nothing like as good as he had been on the phone, but of course he had had a hard night.

I leaned to him. "Look," I said, "you'll just waste your breath dodging. I saw you go in Kalmus's house Wednesday and I saw you come out. Yesterday I asked—"

"What time did I go in? What time did I come out?"

"Nuts. Don't think I can't tell Nero Wolfe, and also the cops, and also a judge and jury when the time comes. If you want to try fixing up an alibi, you know the times as well as I do. This isn't a quiz show with you asking the questions. Yesterday I asked myself a question, could it have been you who killed Paul Jerin? Of course it could; when you mixed the mustard water you put arsenic in it. But the trouble was, Jerin had got sick before you went in to him, and that stopped me, until yesterday afternoon, when I learned *why* he got sick before you were called in. Not only that, I also learned that you knew he was going to get sick, so you brought some arsenic along because you knew you would have a chance to use it. So you *had* killed Jerin, and I knew why, or at least a damned good guess. Tuesday evening Nero Wolfe told you that the man who killed Jerin had no malice for him, he wanted to destroy Matthew Blount, and you said tommyrot, but you knew it wasn't, because you were the man who did it and that was your motive. Then when you learned that Kalmus had figured it out and was on to you, you went to his place and killed him, and I saw you coming and going. So how much did you bring?"

He had realized that his hands were out of control and had taken them from the table. "That's *all* tommyrot," he said. "Every word of it."

"Okay, then get up and walk out. Or ring the District Attorney's office and have them come and take me for attempted blackmail. The phone booth is in the rear. I promise to wait here for them."

He licked his lips. "That's what I ought to do," he said, "report you for attempted blackmail."

"Go ahead."

"But that would be—it would start—scandal. It would be very—disagreeable. Even if you saw me entering and leaving that house—you didn't, but even if you did—that wouldn't be proof that I killed Kalmus. It was after ten o'clock when you went up to his apartment and found the body. Someone had entered after I left—that is, it would have been after I left if I had been there. So your lie that you saw me enter and leave—it's not a very good lie. But if you—"

"Cut." I snapped it. "I'll listen to sense if you've got any, but not that crap. We'll settle that right now, yes or no, and if it's no *I* get up and walk out. To Nero Wolfe. Did you enter that house Wednesday, late afternoon or early evening, whichever you want to call it, or didn't you? Yes or no."

He licked his lips. "I'm not going to give you the satisfaction of coercing me into—"

I had pushed my chair back and was getting up. He put a hand out. "No," he said. "Sit down."

I bent over to him. "No?"

"I mean yes."

"Did you enter that house at that time Wednesday?"

"Yes. But I didn't kill Dan Kalmus."

I sat down and picked up my glass for a sip of wine. "I advise you to watch your step," I told him. "If I have to keep jumping up to make you talk sense it will attract attention. How much money did you bring?"

His hand went into his breast pocket but came out again empty. "You admit you're a blackmailer," he said.

"Sure. Birds of a feather, a murderer and a blackmailer."

"I am not a murderer. But if I refuse to be victimized and you do what you threaten to do I'll be involved in a scandal I can never live down. I'll be under a suspicion that will never be entirely removed. To prevent that I'm willing to —to submit. Under protest."

His hand went to the pocket again and this time got something, a slip of paper. He unfolded it, glanced at it, said, "Read that," and handed it to me. It was handwritten in ink:

> I hereby affirm, and will swear if necessary, that my statement to Dr. Victor Avery that I saw him enter the house of Daniel Kalmus on Wednesday, February 14, 1962, was untrue. I have never seen Dr. Victor Avery enter that house at any time. I write this and sign it of my own free will, not under duress.

I dropped it on the table and grinned at him. "You could frame it," I suggested.

"I have ten thousand dollars in cash," he said. "When you write that and sign it and give it to me, I'll hand it over."

"And the other ninety thousand?"

"That's fantastic. I couldn't possibly pay such a sum, and even if I had it . . . it's absurd. In addition to the ten thousand now, I'll guarantee to give you another twenty thousand within a week."

"I'll be damned. You actually have the gall to haggle."

"I'm not haggling. To me thirty thousand dollars is a fortune."

I regarded him. "You know," I said, "I admire your nerve, I really do. You're too much for me." I looked around, caught the eye of Mrs. Piotti, and signed to her, and she came. I asked her how much, and she said a dollar-forty, and I handed her two ones and told her to keep the change. Of course that was just for appearance's sake; I had given John fifty bucks and would give him more.

I shook my head at Avery. "Positively too much for me. We'll have to go and put it up to Mr. Wolfe."

He gawked. "What?"

"I said, put it up to Mr. Wolfe. This isn't my show, it's his, I only work for him. That last night, me being fired, that was just dressing. You'll have to come and do your haggling with him. He certainly won't settle for a measly thirty grand."

He was still gawking. "Nero Wolfe is behind this?"

"He sure is, and also in front of it." I shoved my chair back. "Okay, let's go."

"I will not."

"For God's sake." I leaned to him. "Dr. Avery, you are unquestionably the champion beetlebrain. Nero Wolfe has got you wrapped up and addressed straight to hell, and you sit there and babble *I will not.* Do you prefer hell or are you coming?" I picked up the slip of paper and pocketed it, rose, got my coat from the hook and put it on, got my hat, and headed for the door. As I passed the next table Fred Durkin, crammed with spaghetti and wine to his chin, got up and headed in the opposite direction, toward the kitchen. As I emerged to the sidewalk a gust of winter wind nearly took my hat, and as I clapped my hand on it here came Avery, his coat on his arm. When he tried to put the coat on, the wind tossed it around, so I helped him, and he thanked me. A murderer and a blackmailer, both with good manners.

Second Avenue was downtown, so we walked to Third for a taxi. When we had got one and were in and rolling I rather expected Avery to start a conversation, but he didn't. Not a word. I didn't look at him, but out of the corner of my eye I saw that his hand was working inside his overcoat pocket. If he had nerve he also had nerves.

Wolfe made more concessions during the five days of the Blount thing than he usually makes in a year. Ordinarily, at ten minutes to two, the hour at which Avery and I mounted the stoop of the old brownstone and entered, Wolfe is right in the middle of lunch, and I was expecting to have to entertain the guest in the office for at least half an hour while we waited. But as I learned later from Fritz, he had been told when he took up the breakfast tray that lunch would be at 12:45 sharp. To you that merely means that Wolfe had sense enough to change the schedule when it was called for, but to me it meant that at breakfast time he had taken it for granted that half an hour with Avery at Piotti's would be all I would need and I would have him at the office before two o'clock. It's nice to have your gifts recognized, but some day he'll take too much for granted.

So I had barely got the guest into the office and seated in the red leather chair when Wolfe entered. I went and shut the door. Saul and Fred and Orrie would soon be passing by on their way to the kitchen with the recorder and tape. As I returned to my desk Avery was blurting, "I'm here under protest, and if you think you and Goodwin—"

"Shut up!" It wasn't a roar, just the crack of a whip. Wolfe, seated, turned to me: "Was there any difficulty?"

"No, sir." I sat. "All okay. More than enough. To the question did he enter that house at that time Wednesday, a flat yes. He offered me ten thousand cash now and a guarantee of twenty grand more within a week if I would sign a statement that I hadn't seen him. He didn't—"

"That's a lie," Avery said.

So he hadn't started a conversation in the taxi because he had been too busy deciding on his line, and the line was to call me a liar and make Wolfe start from scratch. Not so dumb at that.

Wolfe leaned back and regarded him, not with hostility, merely as an object of interest. Of course he was just passing the time until the trio arrived. "A book could be written," he said, "on the varieties of conduct of men in a pickle. Men confronted with their doom. In nearly all cases the insuperable difficulty is that their mental processes are numbed by the emotional impact of the predicament. It is a fallacy to suppose that the best mind will deal most effectively with a crisis; if the emotion has asphyxiated the mind what good is it? Take you with Mr. Goodwin in that restaurant. Since you have succeeded in your profession you probably have a fairly capable mind, but you reacted like a nincompoop. You should either have defied him and prepared to fight it out, or, asking him to sign a document that would remove his threat, you should have met his demands in full; and you should have admitted nothing. Instead, you tried to dicker, and you made the one vital admission, that you had entered that house Wednesday evening. Indeed—"

"That's a lie." Apparently that was to be his verse and chorus. Not a bad idea if he had the guts to fight it out, but in that case he should get up and go.

The doorbell rang. I went and opened the door to the hall a crack. Fritz came from the kitchen and went to the front and opened up, and here came the trio, not stopping at the rack to take their coats off. Saul nodded at my face in the crack as he passed, and Orrie made the sign, a jerk with the tips of thumb and forefinger joined. When they had disappeared into the kitchen I swung the door wide, returned to my desk, and reached around behind it to flip a switch. That was all that was needed at my end.

Wolfe was talking. ". . . and perhaps that would have been your wisest course. After Mr. Goodwin had spoken with you from his hotel room last night, you knew you were in mortal danger, and you thought he was its sole agent. He alone had knowledge of the crucial fact; but for him, you had little to fear. Why didn't you kill him, at whatever hazard? You knew where he was and you had all night. Disguise yourself and bribe one of the hotel staff, any amount required, to get you into the room. Engage the room next to his, or above or below it, and go from window to window. A man in your plight should be able to scale a perpendicular wall of marble by force of will. Any normal will can overcome a mere difficulty; one made desperate by impending disaster should—"

The house phone buzzed. I took it and said, "Archie," and Saul's voice came: "All set."

"Right. I'll buzz you." I hung up and gave Wolfe a nod, and he nodded back and sat up.

"I'm boring you," he told Avery. "What you might have done is vinegar. What matters now is what you're going to do, and to consider that realistically you must hear something." He turned. "All right, Archie."

I pushed the button, three short, and swiveled to face Avery. In a moment there was a faint whirring sound from a grill at the wall back of my desk, where the loudspeaker was, then a few little crackles, then other noises, not loud, which could have been from a restaurant where people were moving and eating and talking, and then my voice:

"The spaghetti here is something special. Better have some."

After a slight pause another voice: "I'm not hungry."

"The wine is special too."

"I never drink during the day."

"Neither do I usually, but this is a special occasion. How much did you bring?"

"I came out of curiosity. What kind of a trick is this?"

"Look, you'll just waste your breath dodging. I saw you

go in Kalmus's house Wednesday and I saw you come out. Yesterday I asked—"

"What time did I go in? What time did I come out?"

As Wolfe had said, a book could be written on the varieties of conduct of men in a pickle. At the sound of the first words, mine, Avery frowned at me. When his own voice came, "I'm not hungry," he twisted his neck to look around, right and then left. Then he clamped his teeth on his lip and sat frowning at me through my main spiel, and when he said, "That's all tommyrot, every word of it," he nodded in approval. But when I asked him did he enter that house at that time Wednesday and he said yes, he yawped "That's a lie!" and bounced up and started for me. I was on my feet by the time he arrived, but he had no idea of slugging or choking, he had no idea at all, he was merely reacting. I sidestepped only because I wanted to hand something to Wolfe—the slip of paper—and he was in the way. Wolfe took it and read it while all that came from the grill was the background restaurant noise when I had been reading it, and he dropped it on his desk just as I dropped it on the table and said, "You could frame it." Good timing. And Avery stopped reacting and acted. He lunged to get the slip of paper, but I beat him to it. I call your attention to Wolfe. If he had hung onto it he might have had the bother of warding off Avery, so he left it to me. More taking for granted. Avery grabbed my arm and I didn't jerk loose, thinking the poor goof might as well have the satisfaction of that much personal contact. He was gripping me with both hands, but when I told him, or the speaker did, that Wolfe had him wrapped up and addressed straight to hell, which I admit was a little corny, he let go and stood, his jaw set, looking down at Wolfe. I stepped to the end of my desk and reached around to the switch and turned it off, and when I faced around Saul and Fred and Orrie were there, in a group at the door.

"I thought it best," Wolfe told Avery, "to leave no loophole." He motioned at the group. "You saw the man on the left, Mr. Panzer, here last evening. He had the tape recorder in the kitchen. The others, Mr. Durkin and Mr. Cather, were at nearby tables in the restaurant while you and Mr. Goodwin conversed. There's no room for wriggling, doctor."

Avery took a couple of uncertain steps toward the group

and stopped. Wolfe said, "Move aside, Saul. Don't block the door—if he wishes to leave."

Avery turned. "Five of you," he said. "*Five* of you." He came to the desk. "You said a tape recorder? It's on a tape?"

"Yes."

"I'll give you one hundred thousand dollars for it. In cash. Tomorrow morning. For the tape and that signed by Goodwin. You can't prove anything, I know that, but I don't . . . All right. Tomorrow morning."

Wolfe nodded. "You see? You tried to dicker with doom. Mr. Goodwin would have declined it, but you didn't know that, and if you had gone ready to meet his terms it would have been ticklish business getting any admission from you for the record. Now I can decline with unconcern. You're right, I can't prove anything, but I can earn my fee, and I can demonstrate to my client that I have earned it—by letting Mr. Blount and his wife and daughter listen to that tape."

"No," Avery said. "Never."

"But yes. Of course."

Avery's jaw was working. "How much do you want?"

Wolfe shook his head. "My self-esteem is the hitch. Quite possibly you are of more value to the world, to the society I am a member of, than Matthew Blount. If I held its interest paramount perhaps I should salvage you, but there's my ego. Like most of my fellow-beings, I like myself too well. I'll be insufferably smug as I sit and watch the Blount family listen to that tape. You had better go, doctor."

"I'm not going. How much will you take? How much?"

"Confound it, go."

"No! No! No!"

Wolfe turned. "Fred. Orrie. Archie and Saul have done a day's work. You have been merely spectators. Take him out."

They came, and, as they took his arms, Fred said gruffly, "Come on, what the hell." I would like to be able to record that he jerked away and marched out, but I'm reporting. He had to be propelled, and, as they hustled him to the door, he squawked, and as soon as they were in the hall Saul shut the door. Wolfe growled at me, "Without dignity a man is not a man. Get Mr. Cramer."

I thought it would have been more dignified to wait until Fred and Orrie returned to say he was out of the house, since he wouldn't want Cramer until he came down from the plant rooms at six o'clock, so there was no rush, but I obeyed. And had a time of it. Some character at Homicide wasn't going to relay me at all, even to Sergeant Stebbins, unless I told him everything about everything, and when he finally passed me on it was to Lieutenant Rowcliff. Of course that was a battle, and I won it only because I reminded him of an occasion a couple of years back when he had hung up on me and we had called the District Attorney, and Wolfe had given him something that Cramer would have liked to get first. So at last I got Cramer and gave Wolfe a nod, and he took his phone. I stayed on.

"This is Nero—"

"I know it is. I'm busy. What do you want?"

"You. Here at your earliest convenience. The man who killed Paul Jerin and Daniel Kalmus just left my house, and I—"

"*Left* your house?"

"Yes, and I—"

"Why did you let him go?"

You couldn't beat that for a compliment. Not how do you know he killed them, or this or that, but why did you let him go.

"Because he was repugnant," Wolfe said. "I put him out. I would like—"

"Who is he?"

"Confound it, stop interrupting. I would like to refer the matter to you. I have something here—"

"I want his name now!"

"No. When may I expect you?"

"You know damn well when you may expect me." He hung up.

I looked at my watch. Twenty to three. It was hard to believe. Another rule in danger, and this time the strictest of all. For years it had been to the plant rooms at four on the dot, no matter what, every day except Sunday, and he couldn't leave Cramer in the middle of the showdown. It had certainly got under his skin. As I swiveled to ask Fred and Orrie if any bones had been broken the phone rang, and I swiveled back and got it.

"Nero Wolfe's office, Archie Good—"

"It's Sally, Archie."

"Good morning. I mean good afternoon. We miss you. I

was going to ring you as soon as I could fit it in. I've been kind of busy."

"Did you . . . was it . . ."

"I did and it was. Everything went according to plan. I'm glad to have met you and I want your autograph. If this is the first good thing you ever did you did it good. If you ever want a job as a blackmailer's moll give me a ring."

"But was it . . . did he . . ."

"He did exactly what he was expected to do. I'll tell you all about it, words and music, but not now. Everything's under control. Just sit tight for another twenty-four hours, maybe less. Of course say nothing to your mother—or to anyone."

"Of course not. But can't I . . . I could come . . ."

"Not now, we're busy. If you can't take it easy take it hard, but take it until I call you. Okay?"

"Okay." She hung up.

15

Cramer, seated in the red leather chair, said, "Skip the buildup. What have you got?"

It was a family party, with Saul and Fred and Orrie in chairs lined up before Wolfe's desk, with refreshments. Fred had bourbon and water, and Saul and Orrie and I were sharing a bottle of champagne. Wolfe had beer. Cramer had nothing, though he had been invited.

Wolfe put his glass down and licked his lips. "It's a preamble, Mr. Cramer, not a buildup. It's necessary, and it will be brief. You may recollect an event that occurred four years ago in Piotti's restaurant on Thirteenth Street."

"I do. Sergeant Stebbins in the kitchen with Goodwin, with earphones."

"Yes. A similar event took place there today, with variations. Mr. Panzer was in the kitchen, with a tape recorder instead of earphones. Mr. Durkin and Mr. Cather were in the restaurant, at separate tables. At still another table was Mr. Goodwin, alone, and the bowl of hideous artificial flowers on that table contained a microphone. He had an appointment with Dr. Victor Avery. Shortly before one o'clock Dr. Avery entered the restaurant, went to the table where Mr. Goodwin was, and sat, and Mr. Piotti notified Mr. Panzer in the kitchen, and he started the tape recorder. You are now going to hear the playback. Have I described the circumstances sufficiently?"

"Yes."

"Have you any questions?"

"I'll hear it first."

Wolfe turned. "All right, Saul." Saul got up and left, taking a glass of champagne along. The speaker was already on. In a moment came the crackles and background noises, and then my voice:

"The spaghetti here is something special. Better have some."

There was no point in watching Cramer; he would sit with his eyes on Wolfe, his lips tight and his eyes narrowed, no matter what he heard. It was more interesting to watch Fred and Orrie, who hadn't heard it and knew next to nothing about it. They had turned on their chairs to face the grill. Fred assumed a deadpan, but broke into a broad grin when I told Avery to ring the DA's office. Orrie cocked his head critically, to judge a colleague's performance, and he glanced at me off and on to show that he appreciated the fine points. He smiled and nodded approvingly when I pried it out of Avery that he had entered the house, and he pursed his lips when I told Avery that Wolfe had him wrapped up and addressed straight to hell. Just jealous because he knew such a fine line was out of his class—followed by my exit line, "Do you prefer hell or are you coming?" Curtain.

Cramer pulled his feet back, not to get up. "By God," he said hoarsely. "Did he come? Here?"

"Yes. After he had heard the recording he offered me one hundred thousand dollars in cash, in the hearing of these four men, for the tape and the statement signed by Mr. Goodwin. . . . Give it to him, Archie."

I got the slip of paper from my pocket and went and handed it over. Cramer read it and looked up. "This is in his handwriting?"

"I don't know. Presumably."

He read it again, folded it, and stuck it in his pocket. "I have known you to pull some awful fancy ones. How fancy is this?"

"If by 'fancy' you mean specious, not at all. Knowing that Dr. Avery was twice a murderer, I determined to establish it. Since it was impossible—"

"When did you know it? Did you know it when—" Cramer chopped it and got up and made for me, and, knowing what he wanted, I left my chair and he sat. While he took the phone and dialed I helped myself to some champagne, and by the time I had the bottle back in the ice he had Sergeant Stebbins.

"Purley? I'm at Wolfe's. Get Dr. Victor Avery and bring him in and keep him until I get there. Go yourself. Don't stop for a warrant. Take him as a material witness in the Kalmus murder, and I mean take him. I want him there when I come—half an hour, maybe more."

He stood, gave me as sour a look as he had ever favored me with, returned to the red leather chair, gave Wolfe the same look if not worse, and said, "And when I go you and Goodwin are going with me. Who do you two baboons think you are? Goodwin told a barefaced lie and it's in his signed statement, and yesterday morning you told me I was better acquainted with all the circumstances surrounding the death of Kalmus than you were. How you expect to get away with—damn you, don't sit there with that curl on your lip! I'll wipe *that* off!"

"I'll save you the trouble," Wolfe said, no hard feeling. "Mr. Goodwin lied to Dr. Avery, not to you. He didn't have that house under surveillance Wednesday. As he told you, he arrived there shortly after ten o'clock, accompanied by Miss Blount, so he couldn't have seen the murderer enter or leave. We gulled Dr. Avery. Since it was impossible—"

That interruption wasn't by Cramer. Saul had entered with another bottle of champagne. Stopping three steps in and seeing that Wolfe was giving him the floor, he came and got the extra glass and filled it and handed it to Cramer, refilled Orrie's and mine and his own, put the bottle in the bucket, and sat. Cramer, who had accepted the glass without knowing it, spilled a little on his pants, glared at the glass in his hand as if demanding how it got there, moved it to his mouth, drained it in three gulps, and put it down on the stand.

He sent the glare at Wolfe. "I don't believe it," he said. "To make me swallow it, try telling me how you knew Avery had entered that house if Goodwin hadn't seen him. And knew he had killed Jerin. Let's hear you."

Wolfe nodded. "That's the point, of course. It's complicated."

"I'll bet it is. I'll try to understand it. Well?"

Wolfe leaned back. "It was an inference, not a conclusion from demonstrable evidence, for I had none. The inference had three legs. First, Blount had not killed Jerin. As you know, I had previously made that assumption, and the murder of Kalmus established it. Second, Jerin had not been killed by one of the messengers—Hausman, Yerkes, Farrow. I have already apologized to myself for my preposterous pretense that that was possible; I now apologize to you. With Jerin sitting there, the tray at his elbow, and with other messengers entering momentarily?"

He jerked a hand to brush it off. "Pfui. Third, only Avery was left. He had had an opportunity, as good as Blount's if not better; he had made a concoction, ostensibly mustard water, and administered it to Jerin. It was credible that he had had a motive; as recorded on that tape, Mr. Goodwin told him that he had had no malice for Jerin, his purpose was to destroy Blount. That can't be—"

"Why did he want to destroy Blount?"

"Because he wanted Blount's wife. That can't be established, since the only evidence for it is inside him, but neither can it be impeached. I presume you have spoken with Mrs. Blount?"

"Yes. Several times."

"Is it credible that she might provoke an appetite unwittingly?"

"Hell yes."

"Then motive is at least plausible. But granted opportunity and motive, two questions remain: why was Jerin taken ill so conveniently before Avery was called in to attend him, and why, again so conveniently, did Avery have arsenic on his person? Indeed, it was not until the answers to those two questions were supplied by Mr. Goodwin, after his conversation with Mr. Blount at the prison yesterday, that my attention was on Dr. Avery at all. There's a third question, did Dr.

Avery know in advance that Jerin would be taken ill, but
that's merely a part of the second one, and the answer is that
he could have and almost certainly did. Kalmus had told him.
That was what—"

"Come on," Cramer cut in. "Goodwin got that from
Blount. He's in jail for murder. He's your client. He's not
mine."

"I'll come to that. I'm telling you why I hit on Avery. That
was what made Kalmus suspect him, and he made the
mistake of undertaking to deal with him tête-à-tête—a mistake that cost him his life." Wolfe turned a palm up. "So
there it was. When Mr. Goodwin reported on his talk with
Mr. Blount, I was satisfied that Avery was the man, but I
had no scrap of evidence and no hope of getting any. I say
I was satisfied, but satisfaction isn't certainty, and only
certainty would do. I decided to test it and made elaborate
arrangements. I asked Mrs. Blount to get all of them here
last evening—all of those involved, including Dr. Avery—
and, when they were assembled, I announced that I had discharged Mr. Goodwin, who was not present, and that I was
withdrawing from the case. I returned to Miss Blount the
fee she had paid me. She was privy to the plan. I told them
that I had discharged Mr. Goodwin for dereliction of duty;
that he had had Kalmus's house under surveillance Wednesday evening and had deserted his post for an hour or more,
and so had failed to see the murderer enter and leave."

"They don't know Goodwin," Cramer muttered, and I
raised a brow at him.

"They do now," Wolfe said, "or I should say Avery does.
From a hotel room he telephoned Avery, told him he had
been discharged and why, told him he had *not* deserted his
post, gave him to understand that he had seen him enter
and leave Kalmus's house Wednesday evening, and told
him to bring one hundred thousand dollars to a rendezvous
at Piotti's restaurant. Of course Avery's reaction settled it. If,
innocent or guilty, he had disdained the challenge, I would
have been through. May I digress?"

Cramer grunted. "You always do."

"It's relevant but not material. I believe he would have
disdained it if he had had nothing to fear but the law. He
knew there was no conclusive evidence against him and
that the prospect of getting any was remote; his having
been seen entering and leaving the house wouldn't convict

him of murder, even if Mr. Goodwin's word were credited. There could have been no motive for him to kill Kalmus unless he had killed Jerin, and the possibility of getting proof that he had killed Jerin was more than remote, it was nonexistent. His compelling dread was not of the law, it was of Mrs. Blount. Would *she* believe Mr. Goodwin? Or, more to the point, would she disbelieve him? If she merely doubted, his purpose was defeated. It was not to be borne. He made the appointment with Mr. Goodwin and kept it. You have heard the result."

Wolfe folded his arms. "That's all, Mr. Cramer. You could legally get that tape only by a court order, but I won't stand on formality. Take it, with the understanding that I may arrange for Mr. and Mrs. Blount to hear it should that be necessary. Will Mr. Blount be released today or must he wait until tomorrow?"

"Like hell it's all." Cramer was trying not to explode. "We can't keep Blount, I give you that, and you're damn right I'll take the tape, and you heard me tell Stebbins to get Avery, but when I get him what have I got? As you said yourself, not a scrap of evidence. You got information that identified a murderer, and what did you do with it?"

"Nonsense." Wolfe was curt. "Just now you contemned that information as coming from a man in jail for murder and my client. Am I obliged to disclose information entrusted to me by a client for investigation in his interest?"

"It's not a—"

"I want an answer. Am I?"

"No. But you are now. You trap a murderer, and you let him listen to that tape, and you let him go, before you call me. *Now* you're obliged to give me the information, and I want it. What made Jerin sick? Was it in the chocolate? Who put it in? How did Avery know he would get sick? What did Kalmus know? Exactly what did Blount tell Goodwin? Well?"

Wolfe turned. "Archie. What was your commitment to Mr. Blount?"

I admit I was slightly keyed. I seldom drink champagne when on duty, to prevent dereliction. "Everything he told me," I said, "was in absolute confidence. There was no Bible handy, so I crossed my heart. If you pass it on to a cop, even an inspector, I'm sunk. Possibly Saul and Fred and Orrie combined can fill my shoes."

Wolfe turned to Cramer. "Mr. Goodwin is tipsy. But his commitment extends to me. I suggest that before you release Mr. Blount you ask him to give you the information he gave Mr. Goodwin, in confidence of course, and probably he will oblige you. You know very well—"

The phone rang, and I swiveled and got it. After the first two words of my phone formula a deep gritty voice interrupted, "I want Inspector Cramer," and I turned and told him, "For you. Stebbins."

In writing these reports I try not to give the impression that I think I can see through solid doors or around corners. If I had a hunch at a certain point, as I do now and then, I usually omit it because I can't expect you to take my word for it. But if Wolfe can break his rules I can break mine, and here goes one. When I handed Cramer the receiver I knew what he was going to hear. I didn't suspect, I knew. I suppose Purley's interrupting me, his tone of voice, his not asking if Cramer was there but just saying he wanted him—anyway, I knew, and I was even surer when Cramer said practically nothing, just listened, with only a couple of growls and a couple of questions. So it was no surprise when he cradled the phone and wheeled to Wolfe and croaked, "Damn you and your lousy tricks! *Goddam* you!"

"Mr. Cramer, if you—"

"Don't Mister me! You think you're a—I don't know what you think you are, but I know what I know you are! Avery stuck a gun in his mouth and blew the top of his head off. Go ahead and collect your fee. That will satisfy you, won't it? Are you satisfied?" He hit the desk with his fist. "*Are you?*"

Wolfe turned his head to look at the wall clock. Quarter past four. He would be late for his date with the orchids.

"Yes," he said politely, "I'm satisfied. You will be too when you cool off. You have been delivered from the ignominy of convicting an innocent man, and from the embarrassment of arresting a guilty man who couldn't be convicted."

MEET
NERO
WOLFE

He's not much to look at and he'll never win the hundred yard dash, but for sheer genius at unraveling the tangled skeins of crime, he has no peer. His outlandish adventures make for some of the most fascinating mystery reading in paperback. He's the stellar attraction in each of these great Rex Stout novels.

TOO MANY CLIENTS 40c

IN THE BEST FAMILIES 40c

THE FINAL DEDUCTION 40c

THREE FOR THE CHAIR 50c

BEFORE MIDNIGHT 50c

TRIPLE JEOPARDY 50c

Buy them wherever Bantam Books are sold